NIGHT FALL
Nightriders MC #4

_____

Silver James

Contact: silverjames@swbell.net

Cover design by *Clary Carey*, clarycarey@gmail.com
Images: www.depositphotos.com
Masculine face with scary eyes © dundanim
Motorcycle in flames © 3quarks
Wolf jump illustration © I.Petrovic

Edited by Gregory Alan

First Print, United Sates of America 2019
ISBN-13: 978-0-9969995-0-2
9 8 7 6 5 4 3 2 1

DEDICATION

To those who do the right thing in spite of themselves.

And, to Roman Reigns because he'll never see this, but I wanted him to know that the moment a fan showed me his picture, I knew he'd be the perfect Digger.

ACKNOWLEDGEMENTS

My thanks to the usual suspects for putting up with me when I got all grouchy during the care and feeding of this book. With their assistance, many pots of coffee, some chocolate, and the faith my readers have in me that I would actually get this thing written, it's done. A special shout-out to Gerri Davis for inspiring the name for a new character, the Club's attorney, Wesley "Wes" Chambers. A big thanks to my beta reader, Siobhan, who always gets me back on the straight and narrow when the story strays. A caveat: Any and all mistakes are my own.

PROLOGUE

Fifteen years ago...

I WRAPPED MY arms around my big sister. I was beyond screaming, beyond tears. A storm raged around the house with thunder and lightning flashes that weren't from Mother Nature. Shadows stomped through the room as I crouched over Becca. I wanted her to hold me, to tell me it would be okay, but her arms were limp.

Men cussed, saying really bad words, words that Becca told her boyfriend not to say around me. Why wasn't she moving? Why wasn't she doing something to make the bad men go away?

"Fuckin' shit."

I stopped breathing as a huge shadow loomed over me.

"Brick!" the shadow yelled.

An even bigger shadow appeared. "What the fuck?"

"That's not a nice word," I whispered. Or thought I did. My teeth were chattering I was so scared.

"The bitch is dead," the first shadow said.

What? He shouldn't call Becca a bitch. That was a bad word too. Then the other word he'd said hit me. Dead? No. She couldn't be dead. She was my big sister. She took care of me.

"Fuck it all to hell," the second shadow growled.

I cringed back as hands reached for me. I clutched Becca's sweater, clung to it as those hands plucked me up.

"Let go, baby girl," the first shadow said, his voice so low it rumbled in my ear like a Harley motorcycle.

"No!" Never. I would never let go of my sister. Something silvery glinted in a flash of light and then I was jerked away, my fists still grasping parts of Becca's sweater.

"Bury this, Gravedigger," the second shadow snarled.

🐾 🐾 🐾 🐾

Now...

A COP HAD found me sitting on a bench at the bus stop half a block from the police station. I was covered in blood—none of it mine. All I had left of my sister was two handfuls of unraveling yarn. They never found her body. Never found her boyfriend's or any of the guys in his motorcycle gang.

Mitch Collins, the cop who sat with me at the ER, who walked me through the system, was a good guy. He and his wife took me in though they didn't adopt me. That was fine. I didn't want any of my baggage to taint them.

You see, sitting there on that bench? I'd started to plan. I might have been only ten, but my sister was my whole world. Our old man had been a biker and our mother a biker's old lady. They drank, smoked pot, did meth. Mom OD'd when I was five and Becca was fifteen. She took care of me because losin' Mom? That just made the old man drink, smoke pot, do meth and fuck every pussy he could stick his cock into. He forgot he even had kids.

Becca got us away from that when she turned eighteen. She was going to community college, going to become a dental tech because there was good money to be made. Then she met Bozo. His name should have told her something. He was a biker. And Becca? She fell hard. And it got her dead.

Still, Mitch and Kathy were nice people. They saw me through high school and I think they were relieved when I joined the Army after graduation. I went into the military to get trained. I had an agenda, one I'd kept close to my chest since Mitch found me sitting on that damn bench, covered in blood, teeth chattering from shock, and scared out of my ever-loving mind.

That was then. This was now. I remembered three things from that night—things that haunted every last one of my dreams: a wolf's head, fanged mouth open and ready to eat me alive, and two names.

Brick. And Gravedigger.

ONE

Gravedigger

THE RUSSIAN FACED the room, flanked by Hardass, Easy, and me. Representatives from every local chapter of the MC stared back at us, waiting. The alpha Wolf energy in the room electrified the atmosphere and the air stank of burning tires. Rage. The Nightriders were entitled.

Russki glanced my way. "Show them."

I grabbed the corner of the plastic tarp covering the conference table and jerked it off. Nobody made a sound, but the fury ramped up so high the temperature in church turned frigid.

"This is Spider, sent from the Hell Dogs as a warning." Russki's deadly voice dropped into the well of seething anger.

A man pushed to his feet. "I'm Ripper, president of the Mizzippee chapter," he drawled. "Spider was mine. Went missin' from Biloxi 'bout two weeks ago. Dropped right the fuck off the radar. Now I know why."

Ripper's face was devoid of emotion despite his struggle to keep from shifting. Growls and snarls edged in around the silence. I covered the body. Spider was a brother. We would treat him with respect in death.

"The Hell Dogs are without honor. They attack our women. Our children." Every eye remained glued on the Russian's face as he spoke. "We will hunt down the Hell Dogs and every club that thinks to align with them. We will not stop until we wipe them from the face of the earth. Until the one they call the Fallen Angel is strung up for my personal attention."

A growling murmur ran through the Wolves. The Russian—before he challenged and killed Brick McIntire, the former national president of the Nightriders—worked for the Russian mob. He'd been an enforcer, assassin, a Wolf well-versed in the intricate art of torture. No one wanted to be the focus of Russki's talents.

I remembered, years ago but it still felt like yesterday when I let the memory loose, when fucking Brick said words almost the same and sent us out to deal some hurt on a club that climbed into bed with the Hell Dogs. They were havin' a party so we crashed it. Too bad there was collateral damage, not that Brick gave a fuck about that sort of shit. One of the rival riders had an old lady—only she wasn't much more than a kid herself. She took a bullet to the chest. Her kid sister was there. Witnessed the whole fucking thing.

Even back then, as young as I was, Brick knew where my talents lay. "Bury it, Gravedigger," he'd said. I was still a provisional, but I'd just earned my road name.

My nose flared as angry scents wafted in the stale air of the packed space—frustration, its acrid sulfur reminiscent of matches struck and blown out, and the hot pepper sauce of determination. Every man in this room was an alpha Wolf. Not one of them would hesitate to fight to the death. More than a few of us were having trouble keeping control of the wolves who lived under our skin.

Another fragrance tickled my consciousness, a teasing memory not even fifteen years could repress. Violets and brown sugar mixed with the rust-tinged scent of fresh blood. I shoved thoughts of her away. I had no time for regrets. My brothers and I were in a life-and-death fight. Too many innocents had already been hurt. Even if I knew where to find her...I severed that train of thought, grimacing as the stench of rotten eggs—my own guilt—washed over me.

Easy's gaze cut to me, his brows pulled together. I gave him a headshake to divert his focus.

The Russian caught my attention with a jerk of his chin. Time to do my job as club enforcer. I raised my fist. "We ride. We hunt. We kill. Nightriders forever. Forever Nightriders." A hundred voices echoed my challenge.

My name is Gravedigger and I come by it honestly.

🐾 🐾 🐾 🐾

Shy

I'D PROCESSED OUT at Fort Leonard Wood, Missouri, the same place where I'd gone to basic training to become a badass 31 Bravo— Army Military Police in civilian parlance— two weeks after I graduated high school at eighteen. And I became exactly that—a badass military cop. I learned *all* the skills and earned a few stripes to go with them. I did three tours, one of them overseas, and now I was done.

Mitch and Kathy were in Lee's Summit waiting to welcome me home. They would have driven over to the Wood to pick me up but I'd nixed that. Stupid on my part, since I was currently trying to sleep in the Greyhound Bus station in Springfield. I'd gotten there too late for the afternoon bus and the next bus to Kansas City left at the butt crack of dawn, arriving in KC just after noon.

I didn't own a car and I'd always lived in the barracks at my duty station. Mitch and Kathy had been generous, but I knew the sting of no money and hand-me-downs. I saved every bit of my paycheck that I could because I wouldn't have time for a full-time job. Not until I'd done what I promised Becca I'd do. I had a couple of vermin to exterminate to avenge my sister. It didn't matter that I was hunting men.

To kill time, I decided to jog down Kearney Street to the Supercenter just under a mile away. It was almost midnight but the guy at the ticket counter assured me it was a 24/7 store. I was half-way there when an angry buzz filled the air. The sound grew to thunder and I had to close my eyes and put my hands over my ears. Motorcycles. Probably close to a hundred of them. I crouched down, making myself small. Just like back then.

I watched them roll past, one man in the lead, then two more and then rows and rows of three abreast. I counted them. Twenty-one rows. Sixty-three plus three. Sixty-six bikers, all wearing leather jackets. And every last one of them wearing a patch on the back—a patch of a leaping wolf, red-eyed and fanged. Unable to breathe, I remained huddled up, my butt planted on the ground, my arms around my knees, face buried against them.

Strobing blue lights nudged against my eyelids and I opened my eyes, raised my head. Cop car. I straightened my shoulders then pushed off the ground, hands out to my sides all easy-like. I knew how I liked suspicious characters to act. I'd give the locals the same respect.

"Officers," I called with a lift of my chin— a silent "yo" from an equal.

"You okay?" The driver held a flashlight but didn't shine it in my eyes.

"Yes, sir. Just..." Just what? Peeing myself at the raw display of biker badness that had just rolled through? I gave a vague wave of my hand in the direction the bikes had gone. "Staying out of the way."

"Smart girl."

"I like to think so."

"Not so smart bein' out so late at night," he hinted.

I gestured toward the west and the lights in the parking lot of the Supercenter. "My bus leaves at six. Thought I'd go wander the aisles to kill some time."

The flashlight had covered me pretty much from chin to boots—desert sand combats, khaki cargoes—non-military issue but comfortable, black military issue sweater and green issue jacket, with a few patches left on for character.

"You from Wood?"

"Not anymore. I separated today."

He turned away for a short conversation with his partner, then he waved me over. "Get in. We'll buy you a late dinner."

I weighed the pros and cons of that. Since they'd appeared so hot on the motorcycles' heels, maybe these local cops had some intel to share—intel that I needed.

"Thanks," I said, moving toward the back passenger-side door. I slid in and didn't even crinkle my nose at the smell. Cop cars started to stink five minutes after you broke the seal on a new one. Gun oil, BO, piss, shit, vomit. Booze, weed. I laughed softly. I was gonna miss that smell. That made me some kind of sick puppy for sure.

"Care to share?" the ride-along asked, looking back between the seats.

"I can't believe I'm admitting this, but I'm

gonna miss the smell of eau de patrol car."

The two cops laughed and introduced themselves. I reciprocated. "Shiane," I said. "Shiane Rourke but everybody calls me Shy."

TWO

Shy

"BURY THIS, GRAVEDIGGER."

I shivered in the late fall air as the memories washed over me. That's why I was lying in the weeds, watching. I wanted my life back. No, I wanted *a* life. I had none, haunted as I was. I didn't sleep easy so I prepared. And now I was ready. Ready to take back my nights, to fall into a peaceful sleep, to put me out of my misery, to avenge Becca. And it started tonight.

I lay low in the bushes across the road from the compound. The place was crazy. Years ago, it had been a train station but with Amtrak and the way Kansas City sprawled out, this place had been abandoned and the railroad tracks torn up. Now it was home to a badass biker gang. I knew their name, and their flavor. The Nightriders.

My dinner "date" with the Springfield cops had been enlightening. They'd had intel that the Nightriders would be coming through on their way to Mississippi, final stop probably Biloxi. SPD and the Greene County Sheriff's Office had cars stationed along every major road in and around Springfield. It had been just my luck that I was standing on Kearney, which had once been the iconic Route 66, when they rolled through.

Nightriders were the worst of the worst, second only to the Hell Dogs. The two gangs had been at war for years and the body count was racking up. As far as the cops knew, it hadn't spilled over to collateral damage. Yet. I didn't add to their intel.

Becca's boyfriend had been a Death Hawg, which seemed—then and now—like a stupid name for a motorcycle gang. The Hawgs were aligned with the Hell Dogs, though they were a small, localized group mostly in Tennessee and Kentucky, though Bozo's bunch had set up shop outside of Kansas City—smack dab in Nightrider territory. I shoved the past back where it belonged. I needed to focus before I got my tail in a sling.

Car doors slammed and girl giggles drifted on the breeze. The Nightriders were having a party. Again. Three nights ago, on Sunday, they'd had a big party out back. I could smell the burgers, brats, and BBQ. I'd seen kids running around and old ladies showing off their property patches while herdin' those kids. Lose the bikes and the colors, you'd think it was a freaking PTA picnic. But that was then.

No kids tonight. Tonight was evidently the Miss Biker Babe Missouri contest. I'd watched swarms of females park their cars along the street and strut their tails to the

meant I could fly under the radar. There was a small bonfire in a fire pit. Coolers were lined up on some tables, along with a row of kegs. Music blared from somewhere and people— mostly girls—were dancing. Everyone was drinking.

I drifted over to a cooler. A guy stood next to it, long-neck beer bottle in his hand. As I approached, someone caught his attention and he turned his back to me. Adrenaline tingled in my fingers at the sight of the Nightrider patch. In my research on bikers, I'd done a quick internet "class" on reading a biker's colors. His name was Hardass, he belonged to the original chapter, and he was the freaking national vice president. Oh to the hell no. I needed to back out of his way and find someone far less in charge and far drunker.

Turning on my heel, I made it about two steps before fingers with the strength of iron wrapped around my arm and halted me.

"Get'cha a beer?"

I schooled my face and turned to face the man I figured was Hardass. He wasn't. Hardass, that is. This was someone new, someone I hadn't tagged while surveying the crowd.

"Uhm…sure." I managed not to grimace because my voice sounded anything but. He didn't quite drag me back to the table but he didn't let go of my arm either so I had no choice but to tag along. I kept trying to glimpse his colors to get a fix on him.

"Draft or bottle?" the guy asked.

"Bottle," I blurted.

Hardass opened the lid on one of the coolers and snagged two beers. He twisted off the lids and passed them to the guy, who snagged both of them with one hand. Then I was hauled off toward some benches set back from the fire and away from the speakers so we could talk without having to shout. Much.

"You're new," the biker said, leaning close to my ear. "I'm Wizard." He passed me one of the beers as he straightened.

"I'm Sh—" I choked off my name. "Shelly," I finished. He gave me a funny look, like he didn't quite believe me, then he shrugged. I scrambled for something to say. I needed to make nice with this guy to get intel. "Big party," I noted.

"Yeah. We're celebrating."

I tipped the top of my beer toward him. "Obviously." Then I took a swallow. I gazed around the open space and managed not to display my revulsion when I noticed a girl on her knees in front of a biker. He had his cock in one hand, the other fisted in the girl's hair and he was forcing her head up so he could plunge into her mouth.

Evidently, I didn't hide my reaction well enough because Wizard growled in my ear. "She wants to do it, babe. We don't force women."

"Yeah, whatever," I muttered. Except Wizard heard me.

He stood and muttered back, "Yeah,

whatever. Your cunt ain't lined with gold, babe." Then he turned his back and sauntered away.

Almost limp with relief, I glanced around, making sure no one was paying me any attention before fading back into the shadows of a garage building. From there, I could watch everything going on—whether I wanted to see all the sex stuff, and there was a lot of it to see, or not. I made myself small by squatting down on my haunches and pressing back into the corner where the garage bumped up against a cement block wall.

I would wait, watch, and then decide on a plan of action. Just like I'd been trained to do in the Army.

Russki

"WHO IS SHE?" I'd noticed a ripple in the air not long after she arrived, and that discovery had nothing to do with any of the reports my Wolves now delivered to me. It was my job to know everything. This woman—and she was very much a woman, not one of the party girls or sweet butts who showed up to spread their legs for us—intrigued me. And not in a good way.

Hardy and Wiz exchanged looks and both shrugged. It was Hardy who eventually answered. "I'd say cop and it'd make sense for them to send in pussy. All I know is, she smelled like rotten apples from the moment she hit the front gate. Rebel reported to me after he let her in. She claimed to be with a group of party girls, said she was the *designated driver*." He made air quotes with his fingers.

I stared toward the garage, made out the shape of the woman crouched in the shadows. "Where is Gravedigger?"

"He's still at Doc's checkin' on Dancer," Hardy replied. "Lucky is all up my ass about the Irishman getting sliced up on the Biloxi run so Digger's makin' arrangements to get him back to Oklahoma City."

Hardy and Wiz both followed my gaze, but it was Wizard who voiced their instincts. "I got a bad feelin' about this one, boss."

I stared at Wiz. "Then why did you leave her inside the compound?"

"Because I figured we were all tuned in to the bad vibes and she bears watching. Gotta figure out her play so we know what to do, right?"

Yes, we did need to figure out her play. I wanted to know who she was and why she was here. "Call Digger. I want him back here as soon as he has dealt with Dancer."

The looks Hardy and Wiz exchanged were not lost on me. "Watch her. Then she is Digger's to deal with."

🐾 🐾 🐾 🐾

Gravedigger

I DID NOT want to be at this fucking party. The idea of sticking my dick in some nameless pussy didn't appeal and that was the whole point of tonight. I *did* want a case of cold beer, my bed, and some peace and quiet. Still, when Hardy called me and told me to get my ass to the compound to see the prez, I didn't argue. You only argued with the Russian if you had a death wish. Still, as I'd ridden through the gate, I got a whiff of something too fucking fragile to remain on the wind long. The scent intrigued my wolf, but I wasn't enthusiastic enough to go hunting.

Russki and Hardy were braced against the wall of the Barracks, the building behind the clubhouse. We all had rooms there and some of us lived there full time. I crashed at the Barracks. As club enforcer, I was pretty much on call 24/7.

"Dancer?" The Russian wasn't big on formalities like hellos or goodbyes.

"He and his bike are headed to OKC. Lucky sent Tinker up in a club cab with a trailer. Dancer can sleep in the back seat all the way. Doc says he'll be fine after a few more changes. Lucky can take care of those if Dancer isn't up to it."

The Russian's head tilted in acknowledgment, but I wondered if he'd actually listened. His focus was lasered in on a spot near the back corner of the garage. Fuck. Someone was hiding there in the shadows. No, not someone. A woman. What the hell?

"We got a problem here, boss?"

"Yes. She lied her way in. Rebel called to tell Hardy. I want you to find out why she is here and then deal with her."

So much for my peace, quiet, and that case of cold beer. "On it, Russki."

THREE

Gravedigger

I CROSSED THE yard, headed toward the ice chests. I grabbed a beer and moved along the wall in the shadows. The woman hadn't moved. Rebel had good instincts. So did Hardy and Wiz. The Russian? His instincts were off the chart. They'd all verified that she was a plant of some kind. Question was, cops or Hell Dogs? That fragile scent, the one I'd gotten a whiff of at the front gate, teased my nose— and my memory. Staying in the shadows, I leaned against the wall, watching and listening.

One of the older brothers, a dude called Buzz, staggered toward the woman I was watching. He had his arm around a drunk sweet butt, and they were looking for a corner to fuck in. A few more steps and they'd trip over the silent watcher. She scrambled out of the way but didn't go far. I didn't move, curious about what she'd do next.

The sweet butt hiked up her skirt and wiggled her ass at Buzz. I heard his zipper, a curse, and then he pushed her to her knees and he mounted her from behind. The sound of a quickly indrawn breath pulled my attention to the bitch hiding in the dark. She'd flattened her body against the wall, but her attention was riveted on the pair fucking not six feet away. The sweet butt moaned and urged Buzz on with a string of nasty words. She braced on one arm and reached between her legs with the other hand, working her clit while Buzz pounded into her. I returned my gaze to the woman. Watching a brother get off didn't do it for me. The woman? Yeah, I wanted to know more.

The bonfire was really going now, the flames casting light and shadows against the wall, highlighting her face. Her lips were parted, eyes fixed on the sex show in front of her. The tip of her tongue eased from her mouth and slicked her lips. Fuck. My dick liked that a hellava lot. Her chest, and man, my palms itched to cup those magnificent tits straining against her shirt with each breath, rose and fell as she gulped in air. She turned, leaning against the wall with one shoulder to better watch.

I inhaled deeply. Cloves and musk. The scent of sex was obvious but there was more— a richer, hungrier scent ghosting just beneath. Aged scotch and brownies. Someone was aroused. Besides me. I sniffed again, taking a step closer to the woman. Violets and brown sugar. Memories stirred, slithering through my brain but I shook them off. The woman was so involved watching—little voyeur—that she never heard me.

Snaking an arm around her waist, I

jerked her back against me, enjoying the sound of her gasp, bastard that I am.

"Like to watch?" I murmured against her ear as she stiffened. She tried to roll her weight forward and I wondered if she planned to kick me, go limp, or bang an elbow into my gut. I spun her against the wall, her face pressed cheek to concrete. "Be nice to me, babe, and I'll let you watch them while I finger fuck you until you come all over my hand."

She grunted in reply and spat a word out. "Pig."

"Nightrider," I corrected, my hand already unbuckling her belt and pulling the zipper on those low-rider jeans of hers down. "And that wasn't exactly a no. That's all it takes, babe, to make me stop."

"Fuck you."

"You will," I agreed. I might have taken her curse serious if the words hadn't come out breathy and her sweet ass hadn't been rubbing against my dick. Shoving my hand inside her panties I found a thatch of soft hair and heat. Wet heat. My nose hadn't been kidding. She was turned on, ready for my finger as I slipped it inside her. She was tight but no virgin. Good. I pushed a second finger into her and worked her cunt, my palm rubbing against her clit.

I backed off just a hair so she could come off the wall and face Buzz and the sweet butt he was riding. I stroked in and out of her as her breathing got ragged. I also picked her pocket, pulling out her ID and studying it before replacing it.

The sweet butt shuddered and moaned out her orgasm. Buzz continued to pound her, the sound of his balls slapping her mound a loud smack that could be heard over the party noise. She dropped her chest to the ground, ass still in the air. Buzz jerked out of her pussy, spread her butt cheeks, pressed the head of his dick against her, and she screamed as he took her ass, but between one breath and the next, her hand was back between her legs, her fingers pushing into her cunt.

The woman in front of me tensed, inside and out. If she hadn't taken it in the ass before, she was at least intrigued. "You want it up the ass, babe?" I whispered against her hair. She shook her head but the clenching of her cunt told me otherwise. The hot cinnamon aroma of her desire coated her skin and I was so fucking hard I thought my balls might implode. A shudder rippled through her and her greedy cunt sucked at my fingers. I finger fucked her harder as she came up on her toes. "Come for me, babe."

She did, her hot cream coating my fingers and hand. I wanted this woman. I wanted my dick buried deep inside her. But not tonight. I held her through the shuddering aftershocks of her climax and once her body had gentled, I removed my hand and did up her jeans. Nuzzling her neck, I made myself a promise.

"Next time, it's my turn. And trust me, I will see you again, Shiane Roarke."

🐾 🐾 🐾 🐾

Shy

BY THE TIME I got my body back under enough control to do more than lean up against the wall panting, he was gone. He'd disappeared into the black shadows beyond the bonfire. I'd just let him finger me to the most amazing orgasm of my life, right out here in the open in front of God knows how many people and I didn't even know his name. What was I thinking? Oh wait. I hadn't been. Watching that biker screw his…what? His biker babe? Was that even a thing? I needed to do more research because I hadn't gotten into the culture, just the symbols. As a kid, I hadn't paid all that much attention.

And what did that make me? The alpha hotel walked up behind me, shoved his hand down my pants, and I hadn't done a blessed thing but ride his fingers. What was wrong with me? I hunkered down in the grass, working on getting my breathing under control while doing my best to ignore the other couple now. I had no excuse for what I'd allowed to happen. And no matter how disgusted I was, I hadn't said no.

I needed to get out of here before he came back for round two. Pushing up, I braced my shoulders against the wall and scanned the area. I didn't even know who I was looking for. I'd never seen his face. All I knew was that he

was tall—way taller than me. Hard muscles.
And he smelled like…what? I closed my eyes
and jerked up my tank to smell the spot where
his arm had held me. Burying my nose in the
material, I inhaled deeply. Irish coffee. The
freaking guy smelled like Irish whiskey,
coffee, and cream. Would he taste like an Irish
coffee?

A shiver of anticipation threatened my
equilibrium as his parting words flashed in
my memory. *Next time, it's my turn,* he'd said.
I froze as icy dread settled in my chest. *Trust
me, I will see you again, Shiane Roarke.*

I hadn't told him my name. How did he
know it? Every fiber of my being told me to
run. To keep running and not look back. I
scrambled to check my back pocket. My ID
was still there. Pulling it out, I had to flip it
over to read my information, which was why I
carried it in my pocket that way—so I'd know
if someone had messed with it. Then again, I
hadn't exactly been paying attention.

Stupid hormones.

This was not the time to panic. I needed
to get away. I needed to get far away. But I
wouldn't run. And I couldn't be obvious. With
my back against the wall, I edged toward a
door. There were far too many people between
me and the corner of the building—the way I'd
come in. Maybe I could duck in the door and
cut through the building to get out. Just as I
reached the exit, the door banged open and a
screaming girl dashed out, a biker hot on her
heels. He caught her and her screams turned

to laughter as she twisted in his arms, wrapped her legs around his waist and kissed him.

These people were insane. I slid through the door as it was closing and discovered I was in a huge industrial-type kitchen. There were long tables with chairs, stainless steel counters, a massive eight-burner stove, ovens, and two huge refrigerators. I didn't cook much so the place impressed me. An extra wide, double door beckoned from the other end of the kitchen. I trotted that direction, keeping alert for anyone coming in behind me or through those doors ahead. When I got to them, I cracked one open and peeked out.

The outer room had probably been a lobby back when this place was a train station. Instead of wooden benches, ratty couches and chairs sat scattered around. A couple of pool tables occupied one side of the room, a working bar the other. People milled around, playing pool, dancing, having sex. What was it about these guys and sex?

I slipped through the door and was about to march straight to the front entrance when a fight broke out over by the pool tables. That's when I saw it—a massive pelt of some kind, nailed to the wall. I looked closer. It was a freaking wolf skin, including the head and paws—replete with sharp teeth and long claws.

With almost everyone's attention on the fight, I boogied toward the door, head down, but aware of anyone who might get close enough to stop me. I made it outside, finally, but had to duck back into the shadows of the front portico to catch my breath. Calm. I needed to calm down so I could walk down to the gate all nonchalant like I didn't have a worry in the world. Once I was on the other side of the road, I'd be free and clear. I could do this. Damn straight I could.

FOUR

Gravedigger

RUSSKI AND I watched from the shadows of the portico. The light ammonia stench of her fear lessened, replaced by the scalded milk odor of nerves. I glanced across the street. Rebel, on his Harley, waited behind one of the cars parked along the edge of the road. He'd follow Shiane once she left. My wolf didn't like that idea. Not one fucking bit. It wanted to follow her. It wanted to bite her, marking her as ours. To hell with that.

After a few minutes—probably to get her courage up, she sauntered to the front gate, gave a cheery wave and a mumbled, "Get work tomorrow, see ya," to the two Nightriders on guard duty. Then she was across the road. To everyone's surprise, she didn't head to one of the cars. She walked down the road, furtively glancing around until she was sure no one was paying attention. Then she ducked between two cars and headed into the vacant field across the road from the clubhouse. What the fuck? From the look Rebel tossed us, he was just as confused.

I didn't think, didn't consider. I wasn't

about to lose track of Shiane. I kicked off my boots and stripped, shifting even before Russki could react. Then I was off and running, nose high, breathing in the scent trail she'd left in her wake. *Find her,* my wolf urged. *Take her.*

Not yet. Not until I knew what the hell was going on. She wasn't a sweet butt. Sweet butts put out all the time. Some of them got off on watching but this woman? I'd bet money she'd never before gotten so fucking turned on by watching. Her scent had coated my fingers and licking them clean left the taste of brown sugar on my tongue. I ran, muzzle in the air searching for her scent. The wind was blowing away so I put my nose to the ground. There. Sweet and sweeter. Violets and brown sugar. The fragrance drove my wolf crazy.

I loped along through the high grass, knowing she was close. Then I heard it. The rustle of cloth. Measured breathing. I dropped to my belly, inching forward until I could see through the weeds. The bitch dragged a backpack out of a cedar tree and shrugged it on. Then she moved some dry brush to unearth a bike—the kind you had to pedal. She unlocked the chain she'd secured around to tree to keep someone from stealin' the thing. I'd known she was in shape from just the feel of her but a mountain bike?

She mounted the thing and pushed off. Pumping hard, she built up speed despite the dirt and weeds covering the lot. I waited until she was far enough away not to notice the big animal trotting along following her path. As long as she kept riding the bike, I could track her. I wasn't worried. She was headed east, in the general direction of Lee's Summit, sticking to the side streets. I could see the light on the front of her bike bobble as she rode hell-bent for leather for about a mile. She slowed then, as if deciding there was no chance she'd been followed. Guilty is as guilty does.

Another mile and she left the street and hit the trails around Longview Lake. This was good for me. She had to slow down to navigate in the dark and I could blend into the wild. She eventually came out on the other side and pedaled into a rural housing development. Big lots, some places even had barns for horses. A few dogs barked but the night was mostly quiet. She wheeled into a drive leading to a large house with a detached two-story garage.

Shiane pushed the bike around to the back where wooden stairs led to a wide deck fronting what looked like a small apartment. She wasn't sneaking around though the lights were out in the house. I settled into the big backyard to watch. Upstairs, a light flared, her shadow moving around beyond the windows. Eventually, the light blinked out. I waited a few more minutes, then went to explore.

The main house was covered in scents—predominately one male and one female. It was quality. I circled the house looking for signs of a security system and didn't find any.

I shifted and picked the locks on the back door, the keyed deadbolt taking a little longer than I liked. On a whim, I picked up several planters scattered around the patio. I found the fake rock in one of them. Yeah. Typical. There was a key to the back door that unlocked both locks. There was no keypad next to the door nor did an alarm blast when I stepped inside so my initial assessment about a security system was correct.

Even in human form, my night vision was excellent. I prowled through the house getting a sense of the people who lived there—a married couple currently snoring gently in their king-size bed in the master bedroom. The guy was a retired cop and with that in mind, I was surprised at the lack of security. She'd been a school teacher. Typical civilians in middle America. There were pictures of Shiane as a kid—but only after about the age of eleven or twelve. Her high school graduation photo, her all dressed up in a robe, that stupid tasseled square on her head. Shiane in an army uniform standing with a sergeant wearing his drill instructor Smokey Bear hat. Shiane standing next to a Humvee marked with the letters MP.

Fuck. She'd been a military cop. Made sense given her old man's occupation. But something still niggled at the back of my memory. I started going through papers in the guy's desk. Mitchell and Katherine Brown. Mitch and Kathy. But Shiane's ID read Roarke. Had she been married? Nothing to indicate that on the family photo wall. I dug deeper, going through photo albums and scrapbooks Kathy had lined up on a bookcase in the family room.

I discovered a series of newspaper clippings. From fifteen years ago. About a ten-year-old girl found sitting on a bus bench covered in blood. About her missing sister, a twenty-year-old community college student, the sister's biker boyfriend and his five friends. About the rental house with bloody evidence of a crime.

Violets and brown sugar. Fuck. That ghost was now a living, breathing woman.

But why had Shiane come to the Nightriders' compound? Why was she pretending to be a party girl? A military cop, foster child of a local cop, whose fuckin' foster mother kept a damn scrapbook about that night. I needed to talk to the Russian. That raid had been before his time, but if there was any blowback now, fifteen years later, he needed to know. Other members involved that night were still around too. Everyone but Brick.

I considered using the cop's landline but that would leave a trail. Someday, maybe we'd figure out how to carry a cell phone with us in wolf form when we couldn't communicate face-to-face. Before I headed back, though, I had one more stop to make. Still naked, I let myself out, locked up and replaced the key. Then I walked over to the garage apartment, and up the stairs. Shiane's place was easy to break into. A spatula hanging on a grill popped the one lock with barely a sound. The apartment was basically one big living space—sitting, eating, kitchen, then a bath and a small bedroom. I could hear sheets rustling and her breathing, but she wasn't asleep. Too restless. The bed creaked. I held my breath. Nothing.

What the hell had I been thinking? My dick twitched and that answered the question. I'd been thinking with the wrong head. I waited a few minutes, listening. Just the gentle huff of her breathing filling the air. I backtracked out the door, twisted the lock and eased it shut. I shifted right there on the deck. A big dog nosing around was a whole lot easier to explain than a naked man. Just as I hit the bottom step, I heard the door above me open.

"Who's there?" Her voice wasn't much more than a whisper.

I froze in the shadows cast by the deck. Wood creaked. She moved to the railing to look over. Don't know how but she spotted me.

She sucked in air and muttered, "What the hell?" She exhaled and in a soothing voice called down to me. "Hello, big dog. What'chu doin' here, huh? You lost?"

No. I wasn't lost. I growled a warning before flashing out of the shadows and heading for the driveway at a run. She didn't follow me.

FIVE

Shy

I WATCHED THE dog run away. He was big, at least part German Shepherd, maybe a Belgian Malinois. About a year into my first enlistment, my LT asked if I wanted to be a K-9 handler. I considered it, but finally said no. I didn't do attachments, not even to an animal. Or maybe, especially an animal because a dog? Unconditional love. I didn't want to deal with that. Maybe I couldn't.

There was no way I'd sleep tonight. I slipped back into my apartment and grabbed a sweatshirt, dragging it on over my head. Settling onto one of the chairs on my deck, I tucked my feet under me and wondered what the hell I was doing. I didn't have time to mess around and going to that compound? Big mistake. I thought I could play them, but I ended up getting played. Big time. My body still hummed from the orgasm that guy gave me. I wasn't a virgin. I'd had guys in my bed. Sex wasn't that high on my list of priorities, but sometimes, a girl needed a little sumthin-sumthin.

What that biker did to me tonight? That was some serious business. I couldn't believe all the live sex going on. No one cared. I'd been standing there wondering where that woman had left her dignity and then, with a complete stranger's hand down my pants, I'd had the biggest orgasm of my life. And before I could do a blasted thing, he'd disappeared. Story of my life.

Biker bastard, I reminded my libido.

I pulled my knees up and stretched the sweatshirt over them. Chin braced, I watched the eastern horizon lighten. Dawn was coming. I'd been home just over a week and all I had to show for my time was the location of their hideout. Except it wasn't much of a hideout. It was a freaking edifice. I needed to figure out how they worked. And I needed to get back in there. The only way to bring the Nightriders down would be from the inside.

Yeah, that was my story, and I'd stick to it if anyone asked. It absolutely had nothing to do with coming so damn hard I couldn't breathe. From a man's fingers. What would his cock feel like? I shivered, pretending it was from the pre-dawn chill and not from the memory of leather, strong fingers, and a scent that reminded me of hot, rich, creamy Irish coffee.

🐾 🐾 🐾 🐾

Gravedigger

THE RUSSIAN TOSSED back a glass of vodka, but his expression didn't change as he swallowed. I'd reported to him once I was back at the clubhouse, showered, and dressed. We sat in the kitchen and a sweet butt was serving up eggs, bacon, sausage and fried potatoes. I sipped coffee between bites of my breakfast. We both ignored the woman. She was the kind who drifted from guy to guy, sticking with one until he got tired of her. She was pretty enough with big tits and a round ass and she didn't chatter. I couldn't place who's bed she was currently warming, but when she slid a plate of Texas toast she'd grilled on our commercial stove onto the table, I gave her a smile. Not many sweet butts would be up early after a party looking after those of us who were awake.

Russki grabbed a mug and filled it with coffee before dropping onto the bench across from me. He glanced at the woman running hot water into the sink to wash the dishes. "Leave them," he ordered. Once she was out of the room, he turned back to me. "Who is she?"

"About fifteen years ago, an MC moved into Lee's Summit. They were a Hell Dog support club, the Death Hawgs. They claimed Tennessee and Kentucky as their territory and decided to push into Missouri. Brick took offense." I glanced toward the main room where Brick's hide was nailed to the wall. That was an old Wolf tradition not often followed these days.

I chewed a piece of bacon, swallowed, then rinsed it down with coffee. Russki said nothing, waiting for me to continue. "I was a provisional when we raided their clubhouse, which was just a house. The local prez was a kid called Bozo. He had five members with him at the house." More coffee to buy a little time. I can't say that night haunted me, but I didn't sleep good for a couple of months after.

"This is nothing that we would not do, Gravedigger."

"Bozo's old lady was there. And her kid sister."

Russki tensed and his gaze fixed on me. "And?"

Another swallow from my mug as I squared my shoulders. "The old lady—who wasn't much more than a kid herself—took one in the chest. She was dead right there. The kid—maybe nine or ten—was holding her. Brick told me to bury it. I grabbed the kid—she was covered in blood. She wasn't hurt. None of the blood was hers."

"What did you do?" Russki's voice was a low growl.

"I put her on my bike and took her to a bus stop a block from the cop shop. Left her there. Went back to the clubhouse and sanitized it. Those bodies were never found. Two days later, Brick and the brothers patched me in."

"Ah. Gravedigger."

"Yeah." Didn't have to explain things to the Russian. Ever. I'd never discussed how my road name came about. Now he knew.

"And Shiane Rourke?"

"Is no longer ten."

SIX

Shy

I STARED AT the short row of businesses in the strip center. After spending a couple of days snooping on the internet, picking the brains—without them being aware of my motives—of several of Mitch's retired cop buddies, I now sat in my foster father's old pickup watching the storefront on the end of the building. Ryder Bail Bonds. It shared space with a massage parlor, a convenience store that sold beer and cigarettes, and a thrift store with grimy windows and uncertain hours.

The Nightriders weren't just a motorcycle gang. They had freaking businesses—a strip joint, an upscale nightclub with very specific clientele, neither of which I would touch with a full-body condom. They had a custom garage called Chrome, a loan company which would be my next stop, and this place. How could a bunch of outlaw bikers get the credentials to run a bail bond company?

Considering how to approach the place, I watched and waited. Traffic was steady at the convenience store on the opposite end, even though it was ten in the morning. Beer, the breakfast of losers everywhere. And blunts for those who got high on the leafy green stuff. The thrift shop was closed, near as I could tell. So was the massage parlor. Nothing moved in or around the bail bond place but there were lights on inside.

The roar of motorcycle pipes alerted me so I slouched down in the seat. Two Harleys rumbled up and parked, both guys freaking handsome. What was it about the damn Nightriders? Every last one of them that I'd seen so far could be staring back at me from the paperback book racks at the Supercenter. One pushed opened the door, so yeah, the place was open.

I fidgeted. Walking in there with maybe one or two guys was daunting enough. Three or more? My nerve deserted me. Besides, I didn't have a good enough cover story. The only thing I'd come up with was asking for a job. Which would put me in a good place to discover any illegal stuff they were doing. But that would mean dealing with the bikers up close and personal.

Time for Plan B. I'd head over to Full Throttle Loans. I could always apply for a loan. I started the truck and eased out of the parking lot. Glancing in the rearview, I noticed that one of the bikers was standing in the doorway. He wore shades so I couldn't tell if he was watching me or not. I'd have to take my chances that he wasn't.

Next stop, Full Throttle.

🐾 🐾 🐾 🐾

Gravedigger

HOLLYWOOD AND I lounged in the back office of Full Throttle. Now that Lainey was pregnant, Hollywood was attached by the dick. Not that any of us blamed him. Crazy enough having a mate, but one carrying a kid? Not one of us begrudged his time with her. We were Wolves. Pups didn't come easy. Even if a mate got knocked up, carrying to term? Didn't happen that often.

Lainey had taken her knocks back in the beginning, ending up hurt and in the hospital when she'd been caught in the middle of a fight at Chasin' Tail. She was dancing for us at the time, then we found out she was studying to be a fuckin' CPA. Brains and beauty. Wood was a lucky stiff. Now she ran the loan company—Sandhog, the former manager, was eternally grateful—and did the bookkeeping for the MC. As far as the IRS and any other government alphabet agency could find, we ran legitimate businesses. We paid taxes and everything.

She was currently out front covering the counter while her two clerks were at lunch. Wood sat at her desk watching the security monitors. The door was open and he could be out front in a flash if anything went down.

The chime on the front door pinged and our gazes instinctively went to the monitor. Wood relaxed. I went stiff. What the hell was

Shiane doing here? Wood noticed and lowered his feet to the floor, coming halfway out of his chair.

"What the fuck, Dig?"

I raised my chin toward the monitor. "The bitch we've been checking up on?" At Wood's nod, I continued. "That's her."

He made three steps toward the door before I snagged his arm. "Wait."

"That's my pregnant mate out there." His growl would have made a lesser man back down. I just squeezed harder.

"May I help you?" Lainey's voice carried back to us. She sounded efficient but there was an underlying tension in the tone.

"She's pickin' up on your agitation. Chill, brother." I squeezed his shoulder with my other hand. "Easier said than done. Know that, Wood. We got this. Lainey's safe."

"Hi," Shiane said, looking around like she was casing the place. "I'm new in town."

"Okay?" Lainey sounded confused, as she should be. I was confused too.

"I'm looking for a job." The smell of rotten apples was so strong it made Wood and me both crinkle our noses. Shiane was lying through her teeth. Wood edged closer. "I have a little experience working with money so I thought maybe, when I saw you were working alone, and—" She gestured vaguely at Lainey's rounded belly. "I wondered if maybe there was an opening or would be..." Her voice trailed off as Hollywood, unable to stay away, slid into the doorway behind Lainey and leaned on the wall. I stayed in the hall watching through the two-way mirror mounted behind Lainey.

"Problem, babe?" There was a definite growl in Hollywood's voice.

"I'm good, honey."

Scalded milk replaced the spoiled apples. Wood made Shiane nervous. Good. I inhaled deeply through my nose, sorting scents beneath the ones created by strong emotions. That hint of violets and brown sugar. No gunpowder so she wasn't carrying. That was good. Wood would probably gut her if she'd had a gun.

"I was just explaining," Lainey continued, "to...I'm sorry, I didn't catch your name?"

Shiane shuffled in place and cleared her throat before answering, "Shelly. Shelly Brown...ing." She offered a smile. "Shelly Browning."

This bitch needed to learn how to lie. Brown was the last name of the cop who'd fostered her. If she'd stopped there, there'd be a trail straight back to him and she figured that out just in time. Still...not like she knew we were gathering intel on her. She had balls to walk into one of our places like this.

Wood's cell rang, playing the theme from M*A*S*H. He had it to his ear a moment later. "Yeah?"

I was far enough away I couldn't hear what Radar had to say but the way Wood straightened out of his slouch against the door jamb put me on alert.

"You don't say." He listened again. "Yeah, about that...Interesting you mention it." More conversation from Radar and then Wood said, "I'm on it. We'll compare notes later." He ended the call and shoved the phone back in his hip pocket.

What the hell was going on? I'd have to wait until Lainey dealt with Shiane, which she was currently doing. "Ms. Browning came in to inquire about a job. I was about to explain that we have no openings. I have two daytime assistants, both at lunch at the moment. At night, we have male attendants to accept loan payments. If you'd like to leave your information, though?" I could picture the innocent smile Lainey was flashing. "You never know. One of my girls might quit."

Shiane backed toward the door. Her eyes had never left Wood's face. "No, that's okay. I need a job now. Thanks for your time." She hit the door, turned and barreled through, almost knocking down the two girls who worked for Lainey. She mumbled an apology as she hustled to an old pickup parked two rows back in the lot.

I came into the outer office and went to the window to watch. Shiane backed out and drove off in a way we couldn't get the tag number, not that it mattered. I'd seen the truck parked outside her garage apartment. It was registered to the retired cop. The girls chattered like little yippy dogs as they prepared to get back to work. Wood walked up beside me.

"She was at Ryder's before coming here. Didn't go in. Just parked in the lot and watched. Easy and Wizard pulled in and she boogied. I don't like her coming here, Digger. Not one fucking bit. I don't want any shit around Lainey."

"I'll take care of it."

SEVEN

Gravedigger

MY BIKE AND clothes were stashed behind an old barn not far from Shiane's place. The moon was coming up full and my wolf was restless. It had nothing to do with the moon and everything to do with the woman up in that apartment. After letting my wolf take over, we'd hunted rabbits and an old coon who scuttled up a tree where he could perch and hiss at us. Now we were hunkered down in an overgrown area behind her garage apartment. She was on the deck again, sitting in a chair, feet tucked in, chin on her knees. A bottle of beer, ignored, sat on the arm of the chair.

The wolf was uneasy, wanting to pace like he did so often under my skin when I was in charge. He wanted to go to her, feel her hands in our fur. Wanted to lick her bare skin. Smell her. Mark her. I needed to leave. Sitting here spying on her wasn't going to solve the mystery of her. I knew who she was. I had suspicions, as did my brothers, on why she'd come to the compound, why she was checking out our businesses. She'd put the Nightriders together with that night when she was a kid. She was curious. Or she wanted revenge.

Radar had done a deep trace on her. After Mitch Brown found her at the bus stop where I'd left her, she'd gone into the system. Brown and his wife petitioned the court for her custody. They didn't adopt, just fostered. She graduated high school, joined the Army. Became an MP. Nothing surprising there since she'd been raised by a cop. Three tours, one in Afghanistan. And now she was back here. Less than a month after coming home, she'd infiltrated a club party. And I'd given her an orgasm so intense she couldn't stand up by herself. I pretended I could still smell her on my fingers.

You need to take her, my wolf chided. *Ours.*

No. Not happening. Bringing her into the MC was a mistake of monumental proportions. She didn't have a target on her back yet, with that *yet* being the operative word. We couldn't figure out if she was snooping on her own or for someone else. Her old man had been Hell Dog before he OD'd, her sister the old lady of a member in a Dog support club. Even so, Nightriders didn't intentionally target women or kids. Brick had been a right bastard where his own old lady and kid were concerned, and he didn't give a shit about innocents.

Claim her.

In wolf form, it was harder to shove my other half out of my psyche but I tried. Did I want to grab Shiane, strip her, fuck her, take her every way a man could take a woman, claiming her with my dick? Oh hell yeah. I woke up at night so fucking hard it took me an hour to jack off. The first time it happened, I'd grabbed a sweet butt, but the idea of puttin' my dick in her cunt? I couldn't do it. She sucked me off instead. I closed my eyes and pretended it was Shiane's mouth I was fucking. That finally worked. I'd have to fuck the real thing eventually. That would be the only way to get her out of my head.

Shiane pushed out of the chair and went inside. I moved closer. The weather was mild and her windows were open to catch the breeze. The shadow of her body moved around the apartment before disappearing into the bedroom. We waited, the wolf and I, until her shadow returned and her voice drifted out to us.

"Hi, Mitch. I just wanted to let you know that I'm going to borrow the truck tonight." The shadow's head tilted as she listened. "No, nothing special. I'm going to try to hook up with some old friends." Shiane hesitated a heartbeat before that last word. She'd been home less than a month and as far as Radar could find, she'd made no attempt to find a job or hook up with anyone. And now, all in one day, she scopes out two Nightrider businesses, asking for a job at one, and now she's going out for a night on the town?

I hot footed it back to my bike, shifted, dressed, and was in position to follow the woman as she pulled out of the driveway. With the full moon, I didn't need a headlight, but I still hung back. She didn't need to know I trailed her.

Shy

I WAS THE world's biggest fool, but I'd been thinking about it since leaving Full Throttle that afternoon. The manager of the loan company looked like a nice lady—a pregnant one at that. The biker who'd come out? He was sexy as hell yet all about his old lady. He was scary but so protective of her that it made my heart hurt. What would it feel like to be that loved? They were making a family. I was making war. It had been a sobering thought, one that stuck with me all day.

Driving more or less on autopilot, I headed to a convenience store. A plan was forming in the back of my mind. A stupid plan, but it was a plan. At the store, I picked up a suitcase of cold beer. My brain decided a frontal assault was the best idea and rather than a Trojan horse, I'd use a 24-pack of beer to get inside the compound.

I pulled up across the road from the gate, which was open, but two guys were lounging there looking all badass and cool. They pretended not to notice me while I pretended not to study them, the gate, and the compound. There were motorcycles lined up in the forecourt, but I didn't see any bikers beyond the two on gate duty. Did I take a chance and try to smuggle my pistol inside? In the grand scheme of things, the weapon wouldn't really matter. I slipped my Glock under the front seat, made sure the hilt of my combat knife was well below the top of my right boot, and stepped out the vehicle.

Making a show of bending over to reach back into Mitch's truck, I hoped the guards were checking out my butt. My baby-doll tee shirt rode up showing a band of skin above the black leather belt looped through my low-rider jeans. I'd made sure that belt was loose enough my jeans rode down over my butt showing a hint of red lace. I owned one set of sexy underwear—the red lace bra and bikinis I'd worn on my first foray into Nightrider territory. Suppressing the shiver the memory of that night conjured, I clamped down on my libido. I wasn't here for a finger fuck or anything else that would lead to an orgasm.

I straightened, the beer cradled in my arms. My boobs were barely a C cup so I used the suitcase to plump me up. If they were checking out my T&A, maybe they wouldn't recognize my face if they'd seen me at the party.

"Hey," I called as I crossed the road.

"Yo," the tallest of the two guys said.

Decision time. Did I ask for Brick or for Gravedigger? I flipped a mental coin. "Is...Gravedigger around?"

The men exchanged looks and I wondered if I'd messed up. I juggled the package of beer which jiggled my breasts, bringing their eyes back to my chest. "I owe him some beer," I added, pasting what I hoped was a sexy smile on my face.

One guy put a cell phone to his ear while saying, "What's your name, babe?"

Dare I give another fake name? Neither of them had manned the gate the night of the party, but that one guy—the one who'd gotten me off standing there in the back courtyard— knew the truth. I probably shouldn't chance it. "People call me Shy," I said.

EIGHT

Gravedigger

SOMEHOW, I MANAGED to lose Shiane in a construction zone. I would have blown past the flag guy to stay on her tail but there was a cop at the other end just waiting for someone to do exactly that. I was a block away from the compound, idling at a stoplight, when my phone rang. Yanking it from my hip pocket, I checked the screen. Easy. I thumbed the accept button.

"Yo."

"You have a...visitor." Easy sounded...off. Not tense, exactly. But on alert.

"Explain."

"Girl. Dark hair. Lean. Says people call her Shy."

"Shy?"

"Yeah. But she walked up to the gate full of sass and attitude, suitcase of beer in her arms. Says she owes you a beer."

What she owed me was a blow job. My dick hardened at the thought of her lips wrapped around it. After that BJ, I planned to fuck her for the rest of the night. Once me and my dick were satisfied, I find out why the fuck she was spying on the MC. "Where is she now?"

"Walking toward the clubhouse. Who is this bitch, Digger? She was at Ryder's earlier and Radar said she'd also paid Lainey a visit."

"Someone from the past, Easy. The Russian's aware. She asked for me by name?" I'd made sure she couldn't see my name patch on my cut. How had she figured out who I was? And why was she looking for me? I scraped my fingers over the bristle sprouting on my face. I hadn't shaved in a couple of days. I'd been too busy following Shiane "People Call Me Shy" Rourke around.

"Yeah. But…"

"But what, E?"

"She hesitated before she said your name and… Fuck, Digger. She was nervous, with a side of guilt. She's lying…but not. There were so damn many scents surrounding her that Bishop and I both wanted to sneeze before she strutted that tight little ass of hers toward the front door."

"Who's hanging around?"

"A few. Who do you need?"

"Someone who can come out the back door and trade cuts with me. I don't want her to know exactly who I am for now."

"I'll send one of the recruits out through the kitchen."

"No." My denial was immediate and harsh. There was something about this bitch—something I didn't trust. "One of the brothers. He's gonna be me for a while."

"What's up, Digger?"

"Not sure, E. Let the Russian and Hardy know she's in the clubhouse and that I'll be switchin' identity with...?"

"Domino's here. You two could pass for brothers. He's back in the office with Russki talking about some shit that went down at Nightshades. I'll tell him to duck out the back door."

"Dom's perfect. Is she inside yet? I'm a block away."

"Door just closed."

Two minutes later, I pulled up in front of the Barracks and parked my bike. Domino was waiting just inside the door. I stepped inside where we switched cuts while I filled him in. The bastard was grinning like a teenage boy who'd just been handed the keys to the local whorehouse.

"Don't fuck this up, Dom. Rebel smelled gunpowder on her when she lied her way into the party. She wasn't carrying but that doesn't mean she's not dangerous. Don't trust her. Don't turn your back on her." *And for fuck's sake don't touch her because I'll rip out your throat.*

"I got this, bro."

I stared at him. He stared back. Dom blinked first but then his hand shot out and gripped my shoulder. "I got this. All of it. Easy, Hardy, and the Russian. We all got this, man. Yeah?"

He shouldn't have been able to read my thoughts, but Dom was one of those guys who ran deeper than anyone ever gave him credit for.

"Yeah."

We headed over to the clubhouse. I slipped in the back door to the kitchen while Dom used the back-hallway door that led to a series of offices, storage rooms and other...places. I stepped into the club room, sliding behind the bar where Hardy stood. A couple of the brothers played pool. Shy had made it about ten feet in, to a round table where more than a few friendly poker games had been played. She stood, back toward the wall, suitcase of beer on the table in front of her. I watched as the Russian and Domino entered from the back hallway.

"Yo, Shy," Dom called.

She jerked like someone had shoved a steel rod up her spine. Her eyes narrowed as she tried to read the name patch on the cut Dom wore—*my* cut. A smile as fake as a porn star's boobs spread across her face. "Gravedigger! I brought that beer I owe you."

The room stilled, all eyes focused on her. I caught a faint trace of ammonia laced with pepper sauce. She might be afraid but she was determined to do whatever messed up shit she'd come to do.

"Sorry, babe. I'm confused. Do I know you?"

She pretended to get attitude. "Do you *know* me?"

"Yeah, babe, that's what I'm askin'."

She blew out a breath that made a *humph* sound and jutted her chin. "Fine. I'll just take my beer and go. If you were too drunk to remember promising me some one-on-one time if I brought the beer, your loss, dude."

One-on-one time? Before I could think more on that, Dom shot back, "You wanna be alone?"

Hardy's hand landed on my shoulder, squeezing hard. "Ease down, Digger." His words were almost subvocal, for my ears only, but every brother in the room had eyes to me. My wolf was so close to the surface he was an inch from making me sprout fur and fangs. I fisted my hands until the claws retracted.

Under control, I was no longer the focus. Now the guys watched Shy. All but the Russian. He watched me, his look both contemplative and amused. The fucker. Shiane noticed that the tension had ramped up but was easing. Still, she looked ready to turn tail and run. Too bad she didn't notice Easy and Wizard blocking the exit.

"Well...yeah. I brought the beer. And if you aren't interested any more, I'll just go find Brick."

Easy moved first but I was over the bar and in Shy's face before he got more than two steps. "What the fuck, bitch. Brick is dead."

The stench of scorched hair filled my nose. Panic. Then the pepper sauce was back. Little bitch was so gawddamned determined to finish whatever the fuck this was about she had no sense of self-preservation. Easy crowded my right shoulder but gave me room to move. Domino sauntered over, the look in his eyes speculative.

"Darlin', as much as I'd love to get up close and personal with you, my brother here—" He clapped me on the shoulder. "—would get all pissy. See, Brick died a while back. So I'm gonna ask one time since I don't know you fuckin' at all, why the hell are you here?"

Shy stood her ground. I had to give her that play. She was outnumbered but she didn't back down. Her gaze fixed on Domino but her eyes kept flicking my direction. No way she could recognize me, but at the same time, she seemed to do just that on some deep level. My wolf prowled close again about to go apeshit over all the fuckin' testosterone surrounding our mate. I rocked back. Fuckin' Fate couldn't be that twisted. But it all made terrible sense. The way I'd reacted to her in the middle of that blood-splattered scene. The way her scent haunted me. And the way I'd always known that I'd fucked up somehow and missed claiming my mate.

Easy, Dom, and the damn Russian all noticed my reaction. Gawddammit all to fuckin' hell.

Shy's hands fisted, then spread, and her body visibly relaxed like she was shaking off her nerves to gear up for a fight. I saw the moment she realized she could die and no one would ever know. "I...made a mistake." She aimed the words at Domino.

"No shit?" Dom grinned like fuckin' Jack Nicholson in that Cuckoo Nest movie.

"Yeah." She edged sideways, her gaze

fixed on me. "Keep the beer."

My nostrils flared as they picked up a new, musky scent wafting off her. Bourbon and brownies. She was getting turned on. Her eyes dilated and she swayed a little, her own nose flaring as she leaned closer to me.

"Goin' somewhere?" The wolf was evident in my voice.

Her chin jerked up and a visible shudder ran through her body. She had to take a couple of breaths, but she managed to keep her voice firm when she answered. "I'm leaving."

"Yeah?" I grated out the word between clinched teeth. She edged away, her eyes glued to me. She'd finally figured out I was the biggest predator in the room. At that moment, not even the Russian could have taken me down.

She kept moving toward the front entrance. I stalked her, moving the same speed, same direction, same distance from her. One step and I'd have my hands on her. Domino hadn't moved. Easy moved away, covering my back. The Russian only crossed his arms over his chest, watching our little drama unfold.

I had to focus to keep my wolf at bay. He wanted to come out, to snarl and fight all these males surrounding our mate. I told him to shut the fuck up. Shiane Rourke wasn't ours. Shiane Rourke was trouble. Shiane Rourke might have to disappear, and it would be up to me, as the club enforcer, to make that happen.

"Why are you really here, Shiane Rourke?"

She froze, her eyes going wide as she finally recognized my voice. "You." She breathed it out, part accusation, part recognition, part...longing?

"Why are you here?" I asked her again.

"I told you. To repay a debt."

"With beer?" I laughed, but there was no humor in the harsh sound I barked out. "Why'd you lie to get in here? Twice."

"This was a mistake."

She backed away from me, stumbling as she hit Hardy, who'd maneuvered around behind her. Shy jerked away, giving me her back, her fist swinging by sheer reflex. Hardy caught it in his hand long before she could have connected with his face. My wolf surged to the surface, ready to rip Hardy to shreds. He held her fist, all but immobilizing her, but his eyes held mine.

NINE

Shy

HIM. My chest ached as I remembered to breathe. Who was he? Besides the guy who'd given me the most incredible orgasm of my life. With his freaking fingers. Standing up in the middle of a biker party. In front of people. I searched for his name patch. Domino.

He was tall enough I had to tip my head back to look at his face since we were standing so close. A brick wall. That's what he reminded me off. A brick wall that I could shelter behind. His eyes, framed by the most incredibly long black lashes, were amazing. Green with gold flecks and rimmed by a ring of forest green, they were intense as he stared at me. Sharp. Assessing. Assassin's eyes. Scary as hell.

I was terrified and turned on and that was so messed up I couldn't wrap my head around it. This guy—Domino—was one of the bad guys. The enemy. Who'd walked up behind me in the dark, shoved his hand down the front of my jeans and sent me straight to heaven. I was so screwed. And I needed to get out of there before I did something stupid like jump on him, wrap my legs around his waist and hump that hard-on pressing against the buttons of his fly.

Backing up, I bumped something solid. Strong hands gripped me. I jerked away, pivoted and swung. I knew how to throw a punch. Hell, I'd participated in a few bar brawls. I barely glimpsed the guy as his hand flashed and wrapped around my fist. It stopped my momentum cold and jarred my arm all the way to my shoulder. Ow. That was gonna hurt like a bitch tomorrow. The guy who'd snuck up behind me wasn't looking at me. His eyes were glued to tall, dark and scary sexy. I glanced over my shoulder and stopped breathing.

Domino's eyes promised death. But not mine. The guy whose fingers still wrapped around my clenched hand was staring at him, not me. Movement flickered in the corner of my eye. Gravedigger was shrugging out of his cut and moving toward our little tableau. He held out the black leather vest to Domino, who stripped off his. The two of them put the exchanged cuts back on, but Domino's eyes never lost mine. My eyes didn't lose him either.

I was confused and then the other shoe dropped. *This* was Gravedigger. Not the other guy—Domino, or whoever. They'd traded vests to confuse me. Why? Did they know who I was? Who I really was?

The hand immobilizing my fist dropped away and the guy said, "Get your shit together. You need to deal with this, Digger."

I didn't move for almost a minute, my arm still frozen in mid-swing. Then my hand dropped to my side, fingers twitching with the need to reach for the knife in my boot.

Staring at him, I stalled. "Why the—" I waved one hand between him and Domino. "Impersonation?"

The man whose name and shadow haunted my nightmares ignored my question. Reaching for me, he declared, "We need to talk."

🐾 🐾 🐾 🐾

Gravedigger

SHY FLINCHED WHEN my hand settled on the back of her neck. Wide-eyed, she braced. "Just talk, babe. But in private."

My fingers itched to grab that damn rubber thing holding her hair in that messy ponytail and rip the thing off so I could bury my hands in the thick waves. Was it long enough to wrap around my dick while I fucked her tits? I'd always had a thing about hair. Weird, I know. But there it was. The longer the better. Spread across my belly as she sucked me off or spread across my pillows as I fucked her. Didn't matter.

She pulled against my hold. "Let go."

"C'mon." I didn't give her a chance to resist. I lowered a shoulder, hoisted her over it, and headed out. I should have taken her to the Russian's office. I didn't. I took her to my room in the Barracks. I wanted her alone. Surrounded by the scent of no other male. I didn't want them anywhere fucking near her. Not until—

I dumped her on my bed, halting that thought in its tracks. She was not my mate. I would not claim her. No fucking way. Wolves had a way of knowing shit like that, even when we were kids. Hell, Hardy's mate had been a little kid when he first met her. He'd totally fucked that shit up and Brick had disciplined him. After he'd healed, Hardy disappeared into the Army and didn't return until after Brick was dead. His unit got caught up in all that Black Root crap too. Men died. Hardy came back to the MC. And now he was national VP.

And that girl was long gone.

When I stood over her at the Death Hawgs' house, when I picked her up and put her on the front of my bike and dumped her on that fucking bus stop bench, I would have known Shiane was meant to be mine. Brick had wanted me to kill her. But I didn't kill kids, especially not little girls with tears streaking their blood-stained cheeks, who stared up at me with big brown eyes that reminded me of a fawn I'd once rescued.

Those same fucking eyes stared up at me now. Fear and defiance. My dick swelled and I wondered how sweet her cunt would feel when I was buried balls deep in her. Shit. I backed away to park my ass against the dresser next to the door, putting space between us. I hooked both thumbs in my front pockets and forced my body to relax. Business first. Depending on the answers I got, then we'd see about the pleasure.

"Why are you here, Shiane?"

"I told you—"

"Don't lie, babe."

She clamped her mouth shut, thank fuck. If she licked her lips one more time, I'd grab her by the hair and jam my dick between them. She was a stubborn little thing. But I was an apex predator and had all the patience in the world.

"If you're going to rape me, get on with it."

The sharp, bitter smell of her defiance clogged my nose, like she'd just filled up a Zippo lighter with fluid. "When I take you, babe, you'll be beggin' for my dick."

And now cinnamon laced with bourbon and hot brownies replaced the lighter fluid. She wanted me. Maybe as much as I wanted her.

"Go to hell."

"I'd rather go to heaven, babe, but answers first."

"Why didn't you kill me?"

"When?" She looked surprised at my question. "I could have killed you a couple of times, babe."

"Don't call me *babe*. Back then. That...night."

"I don't kill babies."

"Coulda fooled me," she mumbled.

"Answer my question, Shy."

"What question?" Now she was trying to be cute. Normally, I'd laugh but not now.

"Why do you keep comin' here? Not gonna ask again."

"Curiosity."

Partial truth. I waited for more, and didn't have to wait long.

Her dark lashes swept up revealing those doe eyes of hers. "Information."

I continued staring. She looked away. "What else?"

Her chest heaved and damned if she didn't lick her lips again. My dick didn't just twitch. The damn thing thought it was a baseball bat swinging for the fucking fences.

"Why did you finger fuck me at that party?"

Now we were getting down to shit I wanted to talk about, not what we needed to discuss. "Thought you were a sweet butt."

She jerked backwards like I'd punched her. "A what?"

"Sweet butt. Club whore. Free pussy."

Her chin came up and the scent of lighter fluid spilled into the air. "Are you fucking serious?"

Nice to know she wasn't so shy after all. "You ain't an old lady, Shy, so yeah. The girls hanging out at the parties who don't wear property patches are only here for our dicks. They don't wanna take 'em, they leave."

Shy swallowed hard and I wanted to bite her throat, leave my mark on her, claiming her. My wolf was all up in my shit wanting the same. "You didn't use your cock on me."

She had me there. I'd wanted to. Still did. I wanted her mouth, her cunt, and her ass. I'd have them all before I was done. Her chest heaved as she read the expression on my face. "You want it, babe?"

"What?" That damn baby tee was strained so tight it'd only take one swipe of a claw to rip it from her body.

"You want my dick? I'm happy to stick it in you, anywhere you want to take it."

Rolling off the bed, she landed on her feet and squared off against me, both fists clenched at her sides. "You're a pig."

Not hardly. I flashed her a smile with more than a little wolf showing. "Wrong species, babe. I eat little pigs for breakfast."

Chin up, she stalked toward me, all bravado and sexy woman. She stopped, toe-to-toe with me. I stared at her mouth. I'd wanted that mouth for days now. "Time's up, babe." I leaned down and captured it, my arms trapping her against me.

Her arms moved, like she was going to hug me. And then I felt it. Cold steel slicing into my back, buried to the hilt. The bitch had stabbed me. I pushed her away, the knife cutting across my side, laying me open. She hit the wall and slid down it. My wolf was howling to get free.

Someone was pounding on my door. I'd locked it. I should go open it but I just stood there swaying on my feet while blood soaked my cut, my jeans, dripped onto the floor. I heard metal clang and drywall splinter then my brothers crowded into the room. Hardy caught me before I pitched over on my face. It was good he was there. He'd been a combat medic in that Spec Ops unit he'd served in. He could stitch me up. And then I'd deal with the cunt who'd cut me.

My vision was going black except for the damn sparklers blinding me. I felt Hardy's hands on me. Domino's. My brothers would take care of me. Then I'd take care of Shy. My wolf howled again as the Russian spoke.

"Take her downstairs."

Shy

I DIDN'T HAVE a chance. From the moment I walked up to the compound's gate, I was dead meat. I was just too stupid to realize it at the time. I was so damn full of myself I thought I could waltz right in there, find Gravedigger, have it out with him, and then do what I'd wanted to do since I was ten years old: Kill him as dead as my sister.

God. I needed a sign stapled to my forehead that read STUPID. Written in red and all in caps. And EGOTISTICAL. Yeah, I needed that particular sign stapled to my chest. What a freaking idiot.

If I'd been close enough, I would have banged my head against the concrete walls surrounding me. I wasn't. I was tied to a chair in the middle of the room, one bare light bulb dangling above my head. There was a drain in the middle of the floor, a table shoved into the shadows of the far corner, and a spigot with a hose wrapped around it. If this wasn't a torture chamber, my name was Mona Lisa.

I regulated my breathing and forced my muscles to relax. SERE school had been part of basic training, but I took the advanced course before my overseas deployment. Survival, Evasion, Resistance, Escape. I gazed at the two men standing by the door. Hard. Cold. And scarier than any Taliban. First and last were off the table. That left the middle two. I would evade—at least in answering their questions if not physically hiding from them—and resist until they killed me. Because that's what the Nightriders did. They killed twenty-year-old girls raising their little sisters. They came in the middle of the night with thunder and lightning, guns and bullets. And blood.

The door opened and the men spun around. Gravedigger. They pushed him out, forcing him back into the dark, dank hallway beyond this room, slamming the door closed behind them. Gravedigger was yelling as the door closed, but as soon as the echo of the bang faded, I heard nothing. The place was sound-proofed. Of course it was.

My brain went fuzzy. I hadn't killed him. How had I not killed him? My combat knife had a six-and-a-half-inch blade, the bottom three inches serrated. I'd shoved it into his back all the way to the hilt, angled up toward his kidney and lungs. And then I'd pulled it toward me, slicing through muscle and organs and blood vessels when he threw me against the wall. I'd watched the blood pool on the floor. It was impossible that he was still breathing much less attempting to force his way into this room. Why? Did he want to kill me himself? Probably.

Emotions crashed through me. Seeing him alive, standing on two feet, challenging the others to get to me. His expression was full of...what? Anger, yes. Fear, maybe. Those should have been what I felt. Instead, the sensation surging through me was...relief. Relief and remorse mixed with shame and sorrow. But I didn't know why. Why should I feel so relieved that my bladder almost let go? Terror, yes, it was there because they'd kill me for what I'd done to him. That made sense. But relief because I hadn't killed the man I'd dreamed of murdering for fifteen years?

I closed my eyes, my right hand trembling. As it had been doing when I rammed that knife into his back. And I'd felt that wound all the way in my heart. Which was stupid. And impossible. And now I wanted to cry because he'd been on his feet, even though there was still blood on his clothes, and I'd been the one to hurt him.

Closing my eyes, I concentrated on breathing, on hanging onto life for however long I had left. Minutes ticked by. I kept count in my head as regret filled me to the choking point. My body would never be found. Mitch and Kathy would always wonder. Just like I'd always wondered about Becca.

God. I was such a screw-up.

The door banged open, making me jerk against my bonds. Men were yelling, their curses crude. A full-body tremble shuddered through me as I caught sight of a massive dog. I'd heard of this, among other tortures— turning a savage, starved dog or pack of them loose. The animal dodged the Nightriders and came through the door. His back and flank were covered in matted blood, but it was his eyes that terrified me to the very depths of my soul. I recognized those eyes. Not an hour ago they'd been staring at me with the same intensity, only from the face of man named Gravedigger. Then the animal lunged, his teeth snapping at my flesh.

My scream echoed off the concrete walls and urine puddled beneath my chair.

TEN

Hardy

THE RUSSIAN GRABBED Digger by the scruff of his neck and dragged him out of the room. Doc Carson had arrived, said he didn't need my medical help so here I was. Easy trailed after them while Domino grabbed the hose and twisted the spigot.

"Hate the smell of piss," he groused. Ignoring the woman now passed out in the chair, he went to work.

We all did. Usually. When the blood lust was up and the throat of an enemy was in our jaws, the ammonia stench of fear was almost an aphrodisiac. When it wafted from the pores of a terrified woman, the signs of that fright now being hosed into the drain, yeah, we all hated it.

I studied Shiane "Shy" Rourke. Radar's background check on her confirmed what Gravedigger had told us in church. Covered in blood, she'd been found by an off-duty cop sitting on a bench a block from the Lee's Summit cop shop. She claimed scary men shot her sister, the sister's boyfriend and his friends, that one of the men dumped her on that bench. No bodies were ever found. The kid went into the system and the cop and his wife became her foster parents. They never adopted her, even when social services discovered both biological parents were dead, mother by drug overdose, father in prison, shivved in one of the countless skirmishes between rivals behind bars.

She'd grown up. Joined the Army right out of high school, went to MP school at Fort Leonard Wood, right there in Missouri. Assigned to Fort Bragg, she eventually did a tour in the desert. She'd separated from service barely a month prior.

Shiane was a pretty girl. Not beautiful. Not soft. The muscles beneath her skin were defined, hard. She worked out—not to look toned like some women but to keep her body honed like a weapon. I could respect that.

Moaning, Shy twitched. She was coming around. Domino killed the water and looped the hose back on the bracket attached to the wall for that purpose. Dom returned to stand behind her. "What're we gonna do with her?"

"That's up to the Russian."

Dom glanced toward the door. "What about Digger?"

That was the question. I dropped my head and rubbed the tight muscles on the back of my neck. I needed to get sucked off. Or fuck someone.

When I didn't reply, Dom pushed. "He's fucking moonstruck, Hardy. We kill her, he'll lose his shit. If that happens, the Russian will have to put him down."

Yeah, that was a problem. But we could hardly keep her prisoner for the rest of her life, like some sort of love slave that Digger could visit whenever he got a hard-on. "He hasn't claimed her yet."

"Did you see his damn wolf? Fuckin' tell me that wasn't claiming her."

"Fate's a gawddamned bitch." I muttered the words, the weight of them heavy in my gut. Nothing came easy for us—not love, mating, or pups.

Shy

I DID MY best to remain still so I could listen to the two men. I couldn't believe I'd passed out when that...wait. Wolf? The guy Domino said *wolf*. Who in their right mind kept a wolf? Oh, wait. I was in the bowels of an outlaw gang's hideout. Tied to a chair. And so freaking scared I peed my pants. Words floated above me. Urgent words. Words that made little sense. Moonstruck? The Russian? Put Digger down? Claimed? And back to the wolf.

A moan escaped before I could catch it. My insides felt like someone was taking a blowtorch to them, like someone had shoved a fist into my guts and were pulling them inside out.

"She's coming around."

I sensed one of the men—I thought it was

Domino—leaning close to me, the shadow cast by his body blocking the light filtering through my closed eyelids.

"What's wrong with her, Hardy?" That sounded like real concern in his voice. "She's sweating and starting to shake."

The scream ripped from my soul. The pain was so horrific all I could do was scream. I fought against the ropes tying me, my body bucking and writhing, caught in some nightmare as a monster bit at me, ripping off hunks of my flesh, chewing me up and spitting me out.

"What the fuck, Hardy! What's wrong with her?"

🐾 🐾 🐾 🐾

Gravedigger

I LAY PANTING on the floor, naked, bleeding, and pissed as hell. The Russian pinned me with his stare. This was so fucked up. I owed him everything as my president, as my Alpha. I'd watched him rip the wolf out of Brick McIntire. I'd watched him force the change on any number of brothers who needed it for healing but were too weak to shift on their own. I was in no position to fight him, but I did. They had Shy. In the basement. Tied to that fucking chair where we tortured our gawddamned enemies.

"Breathe, Digger." Doc Carson. If he was here, I was in serious shit. His voice was like a balm, soothing both me and my wolf. I inhaled.

"Shy..." My voice was ragged and my throat was so dry it hurt to swallow the saliva pooling in my mouth.

No one spoke. I tensed, ready to fight them all.

"She is alive," the Russian said. He'd knelt beside me while I was focused on Hardy. His hand cupped my cheek, almost like a father with his child. "You fought me, Gravedigger." His voice held a chiding tone. "It seems your wolf claimed her and she felt your fight."

I groaned. When Russki yanked my human half to the surface, it felt like he'd ripped out my guts and set them on fire. I'd heard from other Wolves that their mates experienced their pain, that they felt anything extreme their mates endured. When Sam had been taken by the Hell Dogs, Easy had been crazy with worry but also from the pain that leaked through their mate link.

"I've repacked your wound, Digger," Doc interrupted. "You'll need to change at least once more and stay in wolf form awhile. When you shift back, I'll be able to stitch the wound and it'll heal up fine, provided you don't do anything else stupid. Hardy can change your bandages."

"Where is she?" I didn't miss the telling look exchanged by Russki and Hardy.

It was Hardy who answered me. "Asleep in your room in the Barracks."

Relief that she was no longer in the basement swamped me, but Hardy wasn't telling me something. I stared at him but it was Russki who explained.

"She needed to be cleaned up. She was already unconscious so Hardy took care of that and then sedated her. She has bruising and scrapes on her arms and legs caused by her struggles when I forced your change."

Was there some regret in the Russian's voice? The man was cold as ice and hard as steel. Clichés, true, but when they fit, why bother with other shit? This man didn't know what love was. Honor and duty? Damn straight. Respect? When it was earned. But the softer emotions? I had no clue what happened to him as a kid but his heart was encased in a titanium shield.

"I want to see her." My voice was still raspy and I wasn't sure I could stand without help but I had to see her. My wolf had to see her. I was so totally fucked but I was too tired to fight the mating any longer. I'd been pretty much out of my mind with pain when my wolf took over and charged into that room. I wasn't sure what he'd done except evidently, my wolf had claimed Shy. How, I didn't know. It wasn't supposed to happen that way.

The Russian's hand fell away and then he and Hardy hauled me to my feet. It took a long fucking time to walk from the infirmary in the clubhouse, across the courtyard to the Barracks. Thank fuck my room was on the first floor. Domino was there, butt plastered to the dresser that held my big screen. I still growled. He held up both hands before pointing one finger to the bed.

Shy lay in the middle of my king-sized mattress, wearing what better be one of my T-shirts. Her hair was wet and that got a snarl. Then I caught the smell of wet leather and cloth. Her clothes and boots were in my bathroom, soaking wet. Hardy had stripped her down to put her in my tee.

"Medic," Hardy reminded me before I could bite his head off.

And yeah, he was. He'd treated more than one mate, not that any mated Wolf was down with that shit but whatever. He always treated our women with respect. "Thanks."

He flashed me a quick grin at how gruff—and totally ungrateful—I sounded. He helped me over to the bed and I sank down on the edge. Shy was on her side, one hand tucked under her pallid cheek. Hardy hadn't removed the band holding her hair in that ponytail. Her other arm curved around her stomach, pale skin mottled with lines and bruises against the stark contrast of my black tee. Fuck. I'd done that to her.

Hardy squeezed my shoulder. "Sit here with her. Domino will go grab you something to eat. Then I want you to change back to wolf."

I was afraid to touch her. I could smell a trace of the sedative Hardy had dosed her with, but I didn't want to chance waking her. Domino shuffled out then returned a few minutes later with a couple of half-pounder burgers. I scarfed them down, drank a liter of water, stripped out of the gym shorts I wore, and shifted. Someone had dragged in a huge dog bed. My wolf ignored it, climbing very carefully onto the bed and after turning around three times, we settled at Shy's back, chin resting on her hip.

ELEVEN

Shy

I WOKE UP with a mouth full of cotton and eyes all but glued shut by gunk. I didn't move, my brain foggy and sending mixed messages about my situation. I was on something soft, a pillow under my head, a sheet covering me. There was something large and warm at my back, and the pressure on my hip radiated heat. I lay still, working to regulate breathing and heart rate.

Whatever was touching my hip moved and cloth rustled. My hearing was hyper attuned. The mattress shifted. Then something cold and wet snuffled the back of my neck. I choked back a scream but a tiny squeak still escaped. I tensed, waiting. Nothing happened. Well, something happened, just not what I expected. A gentle puff of breath brushed across my cheek, followed by a lick from a rough tongue. Then it was gone.

The bed dipped and bounced as the large animal—and I tried very hard not to picture the wolf lunging at my throat—hit the floor. It padded to the door, scratched at it. The door opened just far enough for a bar of light to offset my night vision as a large wolf-shaped shadow slipped out. Then the door closed and I heard the sound of a lock clicking.

I was still a prisoner.

I should get up. Shake the fuzzies out of my brain and plan on how I was either going to get loose or contact someone who could rescue me. Like the cops. Or not. If the Nightrider compound had been in Lee's Summit, no problem. Mitch might be retired but he still had friends. Too bad the Nightriders headquartered in Mission Springs. They probably owned the local cops.

The room remained dark and quiet. I had no idea what time it was. My inner clock was totally messed up. I rubbed at one eye and the grit on my lashes was thick. Even that movement exhausted me. I needed water but the thought of getting out of bed to find some? Too much effort.

Inhaling, I thought I caught a whiff of Irish coffee. My mouth watered and that helped a little bit. Whiskey and caffeine with a hint of cream. God but I loved that smell.

THE NEXT TIME I woke up, the last thing I remembered was what filled my nose now. I had my face buried in a pillow. I heard the door click and I tensed. Moments later, a wet wash cloth dabbed at my eyes.

"Take a breath, Shy." The male voice was gruff but wasn't one I could identify. "I'm just here to check you out."

Now that was a double-edged statement. Check me out how? The washcloth disappeared as the man commanded, "Open your eyes."

I did so reluctantly. I caught of glimpse of the darkened room and a rough-looking man with a chiseled jaw—a cliché but apt in this instance—before blinding light hit my eyes. Moments later, the flashlight clicked off but I was still seeing flashes and couldn't focus my vision.

"Equal and reactive," the man muttered, like he knew what that meant. I felt him lifting my left arm and then the right, guessing he was examining them. Then he lifted the covers at my feet and examined my ankles. A moment later, my feet were tucked back in.

"You have some bruises from the...seizure."

Why did he hesitate before saying that word? "Seizures don't hurt like that."

"Depends on the type."

Crap. Had I spoken that out loud? Since he was defending his *diagnosis*—and I put mental air quotes around that word—I obviously had. Well, time to assert myself. "Am I a prisoner?"

He walked away. "Someone will bring you food and some clothes. Bathroom is in there. Feel free to clean up." He opened the door and stepped through into the dim light beyond. The door *snicked* shut behind him and the lock clicked into place. I guess that answered my question.

My eyes had readjusted to the gloom and I sat up cautiously, swinging my feet to the floor. I was stiff and sore and the thought of a hot shower sounded even better than food and water, though my mouth still felt like it was stuffed with cotton. I discovered a small lamp on a table beside the bed. Finding the switch, I closed my eyes and flicked it on. Low light filtered in through my lids and I slowly opened them.

A cold bottle of water sat sweating on the table next to the lamp. The seal hadn't been broken on the lid, as near as I could tell, so I grabbed it and guzzled. Man, but it tasted sweet. Okay. Now that my thirst was somewhat abated, time to take stock. In the dim light from the low-wattage bulb, I recognized the room. Gravedigger's. No wonder his scent was embedded in the pillow.

My legs were shaky when I pushed up to stand and a wave of dizziness hit. It passed quickly. I immediately set out to search the room. They'd taken my watch and phone. I couldn't find a clock or the remote for the big-ass TV. I did find the power button but when I pressed it, nothing happened. Drawers held clothes—T-shirts, jeans, boxers—but not the baggy ones someone's dad or grandfather would wear. Nope, these were the fitted, knit kind that would mold to a man's ass and groin. I found nothing I could use for a weapon. I eyed the lamp. It might work in a pinch. The TV was bolted to the wall so that was a no-go.

Heading to the bathroom, I discovered I really needed to pee and I realized two things—I was wearing a Harley Davidson shirt four sizes too big for me and I had no underwear. Double crap. After relieving my full bladder, I searched the medicine cabinet and drawers in the vanity. Nothing but a toothbrush in an unopened package and a fresh tube of toothpaste, a hairbrush, and some of those tiny bottles of body wash, shampoo and conditioner from a hotel chain.

The bathroom door didn't have a lock but the lure of a hot shower to help ease my sore muscles was too big a temptation. It wasn't like they couldn't break the door down. I checked out my injuries. The bruises on my ankles weren't too bad but my arms? They looked like I'd gone ten rounds with a two-ton gorilla. I'd never watched "Psycho" so getting into that shower wasn't scary. I was under their control, and if they wanted to do something to me, there wasn't much to stop them. And for some weird reason, they wanted to keep me alive. I'd take what I could get.

TWELVE

Gravedigger

THE RUSSIAN LEANED back in the big leather desk chair, watching me. Even in wolf form I had trouble meeting that gaze but I did. Eyes chipped from black ice held no emotion. I'd stretched out on the couch in the office when Hardy cut me loose from the infirmary earlier. I might be temporarily out of commission and I had Easy, among others, as backup, but I was still Sergeant at Arms. The safety and welfare of the MC was my responsibility.

"We have a problem, Gravedigger."

No shit, Sherlock.

"You should not have lost control." His voice held condemnation though his expression hadn't changed.

I'd ridden at this man's side since the night of his Blood Moon challenge to Brick McIntire. I had his back and I'd lay down my life to protect him. The Russian had iron control over his wolf and himself. His history was mostly mysterious. A Bratva operative, so the rumors said. The Russian Mafiya. Raised from birth to be a weapon. I'd seen him dish out punishment so cruel even the most depraved among us lost their lunch. All without blinking an eye. None of us wanted to speculate on what kind of training he'd been subjected to.

Being in wolf form, I had a very small advantage when it came to keeping my thoughts to myself. I lowered my head, tucking my muzzle between my front paws in an act of submission. And I waited.

It took a while.

"She tried to kill you."

True.

"Had you been human, she would have succeeded."

Also true.

"I should kill her, Gravedigger."

There was no way I could control the growl rumbling in my chest.

"That is your wolf, my brother. The man knows I am right."

If she was yours, would you take her life? I knew he'd gotten the message when his face went from carved ice to a blank sheet of pure titanium. Telepathy wasn't something most Wolves shared. True mates often developed it in one form or another. Those of us who surrounded the Russian? There'd been blood involved but we could communicate with him and each other when in wolf form.

"I am not you," he replied, somewhat cryptically. I didn't expect anything else from him, but then he surprised me by adding, "When Hardass says you may shift, I will take you to the club, find you a submissive toy to enjoy. Be happy with that."

I knew where this was going. He wasn't talking about Chasin' Tail, our strip club. Nope, the Russian was all about Nightshades, the sex club with a heavy emphasis on BDSM that he'd bought out not long after taking over the Nightriders. I thought he got off on inflicting pain and punishment, but I was wrong. As the top Dominant and Master in the place, he went about his *duties* with the same emotionless darkness as most other things he did. Two things shook that facade—threats to the MC and the mistreatment of children.

Like most of my alpha brothers, I was a natural Dom. There was sweet to be found in a woman's submission, a man's too if that floated your boat. Shy would never submit to me or to any man. She would fight me. And fuck all if that didn't turn me on.

My wolf was up and growling, since my brain was otherwise occupied. He was acting on base instincts. He didn't want another woman. He wanted our mate. And he'd fucking kill to protect her.

A timid knock on the door broke our stalemate and probably saved my life.

Shy

A SHADOW FLICKERED across the opaque—thank God!—shower curtain and I froze. Holding my breath, I waited, fists clenched and ready to fight. Nothing happened. The shadow passed. I breathed again. And finished washing my hair. I was still stiff and sore, despite a lot of hot water, and it was *hot*. Pulling back the curtain, I noticed a couple of things—a folded towel and a stack of clothes. Good to know that shadow hadn't been my imagination. Even better, the shadow hadn't meant me any harm.

I dried off before taking the clothes over to the bed to check them out. There was a pair of sweatpants, a package of cotton panties—bikinis—plus a sports bra, and a long-sleeved Harley T-shirt. Everything was new but the tee. It wasn't as big as the one I'd worn that belonged to Gravedigger and it held a faint floral scent. I sniffed deeply, sort of pissed. Did he keep women's clothes around? My nose identified the scent—a well-known fabric sheet. So, it was almost fresh from the dryer. Good to know.

Stupid me. Why should I care if he kept women? Only I did. The thought of him with another woman turned me inside out. I wanted to pound my fists against him. I wanted to throw up. I wanted…to breathe. I stopped obsessing and bent over at the waist, inhaling great gulps of air. Another stupid move because I'd hyperventilate if I kept this up.

As I regained control, I noticed my forearms. The crosshatch of bruising was testament to what the Nightriders had done to me. I'd been tied up, believing they planned to torture me, before or after raping me, and then they would kill me. Because I'd tried to kill Gravedigger. Their brother. It was all about the biker brotherhood and their twisted code of honor.

I threw up a little in my mouth. The thought of the big, scary biker dead—at my hand—was enough to send me back into the bathroom. I knelt beside the toilet dry heaving. What the freaking hell was wrong with me? He and the Nightriders murdered my sister. They ripped my life into bloody strips that they flung into the wind like confetti streamers.

Except they hadn't killed me. Well, Gravedigger hadn't. I didn't think about it back then, but as an adult, that night haunted me. I could still hear that growling voice say, "Bury this, Gravedigger." Brick. Whose name made these people exchange weird looks. Gravedigger's vest had a sergeant at arms patch. I knew what that meant in biker speak. He was the enforcer for the MC. Except he'd been fifteen years younger that night. Too young for that kind of position. Still, Brick had meant for him to bury *me.*

Except. Digger left me sitting on a bench a block from the police station. He could have killed me. Or dumped me anywhere, but he didn't. And rather than ending up in the system, Mitch and Kathy had taken me in. They'd looked after me. Given me stability. A home where food was plentiful, I went to school every day, I had clean clothes, and a bed I didn't have to share with anyone. A place where I wasn't scared every minute of every day and night.

Where was the bad nasty biker in the decision Gravedigger had made?

"You gonna stay down there all day, babe?"

I jerked and banged my head on the toilet. "Ow!" I'd stopped heaving and lost in my memories, I'd curled up around it because the cool porcelain felt good against my throbbing head.

"Need some ice?"

I glared up at the man. Hardass. The MC's VP. Crap. Before I could move, he'd grabbed my arms. Though I did my best to jerk away, his grip was unyielding, yet also gentle. He checked my arms, top and bottom, then he gazed into my eyes.

"Blink."

"What?"

"Blink."

I blinked.

"Still no signs of a concussion."

"How would you know?"

"I was a combat medic. Among other things."

I blink-blinked. Whoa. *Other things?* I knew what that meant. Special operations. And I'd just thought these guys were scary before. "Good to know," I whispered.

🐾 🐾 🐾 🐾

Gravedigger

BEFORE THE RUSSIAN said anything, the door eased open and a mop of curly, blonde hair poked through the crack. A tiny body followed. Noni Prescott, the little girl Easy and his old lady were raising as their own. Technically, the kid was Sam's niece. She held one pudgy finger to her lips and slipped into the office, closing the door behind her.

She tiptoed—literally standing on her toes—over to the couch. She pointed at the scabbed-over wound on my back and side. "Owie, Didger. I sowwy." Then she kissed me on the nose and awkwardly patted my head.

I licked her cheek. Noni was a sweet kid who'd seen far too much violence in her young life. The Hell Dogs killed her mom, wanting to kidnap Noni and her older brother Jonah. He'd gotten them to the compound looking for Easy, and the girl had latched onto Russki, something that still blew me away. The Russian was not a warm and fuzzy kind of guy who put up with kids. All except Noni. And maybe Jonah. And Louie and Levi, the twin troublemakers who were Lainey's little brothers. Okay, being honest, the Russian had a thing about kids. Noni patted me again, then toddled over to Russki, holding her arms out.

"Up, Roo," she demanded. He lifted her onto his lap. She straddled him, face-to-face. Her pudgy toddler hands cupped his face and she patted his cheeks. "Roo?"

"*Da?*"

"Hide." The word came out as a whisper.

THIRTEEN

Russki

THE DOOR TO my office crashed open. Noni's eyes widened, but not in fear. The man standing there didn't look panicked but urgency coated his voice.

"We have a situation, boss."

Smoke Jenner was not a man who panicked. He had been a nomad for years, a man I trusted with my life, and the life of all our brothers. Smoke found his mate, a woman who had been an arson investigator. Now she rode the back of his bike. The world made for strange pairings. I glanced at Gravedigger. Very strange indeed.

I stood, carrying Noni to the couch and setting her down beside the wolf. He would guard her with his life. It would take more than one bullet to stop him, even severely injured. "Stay here." The order included both of them. The wolf growled, then nosed Noni. She sank one hand into his ruff. I wasn't sure who the gesture was meant to comfort. I followed Smoke out, shutting the door behind me.

Stepping into the main room was like walking onto a movie set. Men in black and camouflage, all armed and covered in Kevlar, spread in a semicircle just inside the room. A handful of Nightriders stood facing them from various positions, everyone loose and ready to fight. One man appeared to be more in charge and I read the capital letters stenciled on his bullet-proof vest with interest. ICE.

"You're the ones who came barging in without an invitation," Easy was saying. With a broad smile on his face that fooled no one due to the ice in his Siberian Husky eyes. "You need to explain why you're here, what you're lookin' for, and you better have a paper all signed, sealed, and delivered before you take one more step."

"Are you threatenin' us, boy?" A local LEO barged to the front of the line, glaring at Easy. We knew this cop, all too well.

Easy held his hands out at his sides. "I'm not the one standing on private property armed to the teeth, Deputy Dickwad."

The man puffed up even more and made it two steps before the man with ICE on his chest stuck out an arm and stopped him. "I'm Agent Nelson. We have a warrant for Sergei…" His voice trailed off as he glanced at the paper in his hand. His lips moved as he practiced my surname.

I saved him the trouble. "Rusakovavich."

All eyes swung to me and I watched with amusement as the intruders stiffened. The air thickened with the scent of ammonia. I offered a smile any smart cop would understand was mocking.

"We have a warrant for your arrest for violation of the immigration laws of the United States."

"Is this so?" I was mildly amused.

"You are in this country illegally."

"I am?" I had citizenship papers that stated otherwise but I was in the mood to play.

The deputy poked a finger into thin air. "We got evidence that you sumbitches are involved in human trafficking, including sellin' women to the sex trade."

This charge was ludicrous, though problematic given the presence of Shiane Rourke in the Barracks. Smoke already had his phone out, texting Hardy. All of my Wolves turned their gazes on the deputy. He'd developed a hard-on for the Nightriders the moment he'd been assigned to the Mission Springs substation.

"I assure you, Agent Nelson, I am a naturalized citizen of the United States. I can supply certified copies of my papers. As for your other charge—"

Every cop in the place tensed and fingers squeezed weapons suddenly coming up to bear on all of us. A tiny blur burst from the hallway behind me, followed by a very large and very angry black wolf. Noni was a little monkey. She scampered up the back of my leg and onto my back until her arms were around my neck, little legs clenching my sides. They weren't long enough to circle my torso. Gravedigger slid to a stop beside me, lips pulled up in a snarl showing off all his teeth. I dropped my hand to the top of his head.

Noni, nose crinkled and eyes slitted, glowered at the LEOs. "My Roo!" she declared.

As if they'd been waiting for their cue, the door to the kitchen opened and several of the old ladies emerged. Sam, who was mated to Easy and was Noni's guardian, stopped dead. Lainey, Ginger, and Leigh all but knocked her over.

"What's going on here?" Leigh sounded like the arson investigator she used to be. She stepped around Sam and stared down the men. I smirked. My Wolves who were mated had found strong women.

"Show us your hands!" Weapons cocked.

"Oh, for crissakes," Sam muttered, but she held her hands out at her hips, palms facing the men.

Smoke drawled, "The bastards claim to have evidence that we're trafficking women for sex."

"Smoke!" Sam chastised and dipped her head toward me and the monkey on my back. "Little ears."

Leigh rolled her eyes at her mate. "At least he didn't use the f-word, Sam. Be grateful for small favors."

"We have a warrant," the ICE agent reminded, though he was looking perplexed. The women arrayed against him likely did not fit the portrait he had in his head of what club whores would look like. That was because these were old ladies. Sam had worked search and rescue for the ski patrol in Utah. Leigh, an investigator for the Dallas Fire Department. Lainey, a CPA. Ginger was the only one who might fit his preconceived notions, though she could hold her own with the others.

"I've called our attorney," Lainey said. "We'll just wait until he gets here."

"Fine," Deputy Dickwad snarled, then he spoke into his radio, requesting animal control.

Gravedigger growled and Noni shook her finger at the cop. "*My* Didger!" She shimmied down and landed on the wolf's back. He didn't move as she wrapped her arms around his neck, straddling him like a he was a small pony. "Mine," she said again, glowering. "Not yours!"

"That's a fuckin' wolf!"

"No cussing!" Four female voices barked the order at the same time. "Little ears," Sam's solo voice added.

My brothers choked on their laughter. I also felt the need to press my lips together. Under normal circumstances, the women would not act this way. They knew their place and their mates would have words for them later. The women would apologize and then I would laugh with them. My brothers were not pussy whipped but their women weren't cocked up either.

The women's presence was problematic. Had they somehow heard of the situation with Gravedigger? He was not one to mix with the old ladies. He did not have the easy ways of many of the Wolves. He was my enforcer, the one who carried out my orders with no hesitation. No matter what those orders decreed. He remained aloof from the women. And from his brothers as well, I realized. It took a special kind of man to kill another, especially when that other had once been a brother. It occurred to me that my enforcer was far more like me than I had realized. Until this moment.

Now, he had a woman, one who was the other half of his soul. Any of the Wolves would dispose of her for what she had done to Gravedigger, but the act would profoundly change the life of the Club. No, if Shiane Rourke was to die, she would do so by my hand.

The cops closest to the door stirred as it opened and one of their own inserted his head to yell out, "There's a guy out here claiming to be legal counsel."

"Let him in," the ICE agent ordered.

Wesley Chambers strolled through the door like he was walking into a five-star restaurant. His suit easily cost five figures, his custom western boots another five. Silver glinted at his temples but his unlined face could belong to a man anywhere from thirty-five to fifty. Good genetics guaranteed he would keep both his looks and virility well past middle age. The attorney was an alpha Wolf who found his prey in the courtroom.

He strode directly to Agent Nelson and

traded his business card for the warrant. "I'm Wesley Chambers. I represent the Nightriders Motorcycle Club in general and Sergei Rusakovavich specifically." The man was a speed reader so it didn't take him long to deal with the warrant. Placing his leather briefcase on the nearest table, he opened it and withdrew a file. He offered it to the ICE agent with a wolf's smile. "These papers will verify Mr. Rusakovavich's immigration and citizenship status."

Chambers paused while the agent read the file. The moment Nelson's eyes flicked up to meet his, our very crafty attorney continued. "As for the other allegations, the Nightriders Motorcycle Club owns several business enterprises, none of which involve any illegal activities. While two of those enterprises do involve—" He paused dramatically with a telling look toward Noni. "*Adult* entertainment, both are completely above board. All employees are free to come and go at their will. They are paid wages and also receive tips. The Nightriders pay employment taxes on those wages and there are benefits, including health care and tuition reimbursement." His wolf's grin returned. "I can personally attest to that last perk. My current legal assistant danced at Chasin' Tail while going to college."

With a sweep of his hand, Chambers encompassed the old ladies and Noni. "These ladies and the child are family members. I doubt their husbands would allow them to be on property if there was nefarious trafficking occurring."

"Where the hell is Shiane Rourke?"

Sam hissed under her breath and raised one finger as she stepped toward the deputy. Easy caught her around the waist. "Babe," he urged under his breath. She stilled but her body vibrated within his hold.

"Who?" It was time for me to take back control.

The deputy thrust out his chest and swaggered a few steps toward me. Agent Nelson halted his forward momentum if not the man's mouth.

"You know who I'm talkin' about. Her daddy's truck was parked across the street."

"Does it remain parked there?"

"You know it's gone, you sonava—"

"Language, deputy." Nelson 's voice was soft but compelling. This man could become a problem. Under normal conditions, I would assign Gravedigger to investigate the agent. We had other things to deal with first.

My smile was every bit as predatory as Chambers' had been. "Perhaps you should check with Ms. Rourke's foster father, who is the legal owner of the truck. I believe it is currently parked in his driveway."

FOURTEEN

Shy

I RINSED OUT my mouth and splashed
water on my face. The guy named Hardass
remained out in the bedroom, shoulder
leaning against the bathroom door frame. He
spent a lot of time reading incoming texts on
his phone, but I had no doubt that he was fully
aware of my activities. I opened the
toothbrush I'd noticed before and used it.
Hardass was still glued to his phone.

To get out of the bathroom, I'd have to
squeeze past him. Unless he moved. "Can I
get by you?"

"I don't know. *Can* you?"

I rolled my eyes. Who was this guy to
lecture me on proper grammar? "May I get
past you, sir?" I asked with as much sarcasm
as I could muster.

"Sure." He backed away giving me just
enough room to dodge him without touching.

I sank onto the edge of the bed. After a
period of silence lasting far longer than was
comfortable, I broke it. "What now?"

He read the latest text then raised his
eyes to study me. I found no compassion there,
despite the gentle way he'd handled me

earlier. Not sure I could blame him, given the circumstances.

"Now you make a decision."

I did not like the sound of that. Not one little bit but I nodded, knowing I needed to hear him out.

"You have one chance, babe."

There was nothing friendly in his voice. Saliva pooled in my mouth and the look on his face made me want to pee my pants. I swallowed hard and dipped my chin just a hair to indicate he should continue. No way could I speak out loud and I was too terrified to move. Hardass looked like he was a millisecond away from ripping off my head.

"The clubhouse is being raided. It's all bogus but there's a deputy who insists that we kidnapped you."

I sucked in a breath. Rescue!

"Except we didn't. You walked in here of your own free will."

Okay, technically that was true but they'd imprisoned me and I was still a prisoner.

"And then you attempted to murder one of our brothers. It wasn't self-defense because he was unarmed, and you didn't have a mark on you until *after* you stabbed and slashed him."

I stopped breathing because that was also technically true. But in the MC's world, they would deal with that crime in-house. No way would they involve the cops. Except the cops were here and I was being blackmailed into doing whatever it was they wanted. He must have seen something on my face leading him to believe I understood my situation. He continued.

"I'm going to walk you into the clubhouse. You will explain that you came here of your own free will. You will explain that you drove your foster father's truck back to his house and you came back here, of your own free will, on the back of my bike. You will then convince them that you are fine and wish to stay here."

I had to clear my throat but I managed to croak out, "And if I don't?"

"We'll press charges and turn over all our evidence."

A snorting laugh escaped but trailed off as I took in his expression. He was dead serious, and I was afraid that the operative word was "dead." As in, I would be.

"We're law-abiding citizens, Shiane. There's a bloody knife with your fingerprints and the bloody clothing you were wearing."

Holding out my arms, I tried to sneer at him. "And how do you explain these bruises?"

"We had to restrain you while waiting for the authorities to arrive."

He was so damn sure of himself. "Except I've been here over forty-eight hours. And there was no report filed."

The corner of his mouth ticked up in a smile that more closely resembled a snarl. "Do you really think we can't cover ourselves?" His eyes were glacial as he added, "As a former MP, you know all sorts of accidents happen to incarcerated prisoners."

Crap. That wasn't a veiled threat. That

was the truth. If I ended up in jail, they'd arrange for me to never walk out breathing. I'd be carried out in a body bag.

Another text dinged on his phone and he glanced down. "You have thirty seconds to decide," he said without looking up.

"Fine."

"Fine?"

"I'll lie to the cops."

"Not a lie if it's the truth, babe."

Three minutes later, we walked through the door between the kitchen and the club room. I wore the long-sleeved T-shirt to cover my arms. Hardass kept his arm around my neck, effectively chaining me to his side. Guns cocked as we entered the room and we both halted. I saw four women, one of them the pregnant manager of the loan company. The cops were in a face-off with the MC brothers. Then I saw the little girl sitting on the back of a huge black dog—the same one that had charged me in the basement and then curled up in bed with me later, only I'd thought the animal had been a wolf. I considered pinching myself because this had to be a bad dream.

"Who are you?" a tall man wearing an ICE bulletproof vest barked at me.

"Shy—" I cleared my throat and spoke louder. "Shiane Rourke. What's going on?"

Gravedigger

HAD NONI NOT been riding me, I would have gone for Hardy's throat. Seeing his arm wrapped around Shy fucked with my brain big time. But Noni was wrapped around me and there was no fucking way I'd harm that kid, so there I stood, vibrating with the need to taste the blood of my brother for touching my mate. The Russian stroked my head and my wolf settled, just a little.

The ICE agent stared at Shy, assessing her body language. She was tense, uncomfortable in Hardy's hold. "We had information that you'd been kidnapped, Ms. Rourke."

"I wanna know why your daddy's truck is back at his house and no one saw you come back," the deputy interrupted. "What are you doin' here with these bastards?"

I noticed Hardy's arm tighten around her neck. She swallowed, then her shoulders straightened. "I came to see an old army buddy," Shy said. "I thought Mitch might need his truck so I took it home and rode back here with…him." She indicated Hardy with a subtle tilt of her head.

"Are we to understand that you're here of your own free will?" Agent Nelson cut the deputy off.

"I am."

Every one of us could smell the lie. And her fear. Rotten apples and ammonia weren't a good mix, except for now. I got the feeling she'd lie her pretty little ass off to keep the cops from going down. Because they would and she was smart enough to realize that if she gave anything away, not one of them would leave this compound alive. I relaxed. She was a good little soldier. Once I fully claimed her, she'd make an amazing old lady.

"You were a military police officer?" Nelson kept pushing.

"Yes, sir."

"And you're comfortable—"

"I am." She rushed to answer. "You are aware that the Nightriders have several legitimate businesses. I heard what you said about human trafficking. I don't believe that has or is occurring."

Conviction. Yeah, she believed that we weren't running women. We didn't. If the girls at Chasin' Tail wanted to make extra money, they took the prostitution off premises and on their own time. Hell, since Hollywood's old lady took over the bookkeeping, we even instituted a damned tuition reimbursement plan for the dancers. We looked like real citizens on paper. That said, just because we didn't currently run women for the sex trade didn't meant the Club hadn't in the past. I glanced at the hide on the wall. Brick had been a fucking bastard with no regard for anyone or anything.

Nelson's gaze roamed the room and his next words filled the place with a tension so thick no one breathed.

"You can leave with us now, Ms. Rourke."

FIFTEEN

Shy

MY VISION GRAYED out. My rescue was right here, waiting for me to grab it. It would be my word against the Nightriders as to what actually happened between Gravedigger and me. Except I suddenly realized Hardass had lied to me. They wouldn't turn me over to the cops. In fact, the cops would die. Some of the Nightriders would as well—maybe even the old ladies or the little girl. I knew in my gut that none of the cops would go home to their families. I wanted to throw up. I wanted to fight. I wanted to curl up in the fetal position and bawl my eyes out. I couldn't do any of those things. I had a heartbeat, maybe two to answer.

"S'all cool, sir. Like I said, just catching up with an old buddy."

The agent's hand rested on the butt of his pistol and the local deputy looked like he was ready to pull the trigger of the riot shotgun he carried. "Are you sure, Ms. Rourke?"

I was sure we'd all die if I said no. "I'm sure. I'm fine."

And just like that, oxygen rushed back into the room and everyone took a breath. I realized that all the cops felt the same hostility I'd felt. Thank God none of them had twitchy fingers. Except the deputy. I watched in horror as he brought the shotgun up, pointing it not at Hardass and me but at the club president, the dog and the little girl.

In a moment of pure terror, all the air was sucked from the room, and it was like watching a movie when the action sequence goes into slow motion. The dog twisted his head, teeth grabbing the girl's shirt, ripping her off his back, then he had her under him, his body covering hers—like he knew exactly what was happening. The Russian guy wearing the president's patch stepped in front of them, shielding them with his body. The women screamed and while I knew I was hearing noise, it—like the scene—undulated so the words were unintelligible. And suddenly the guy called Easy was there, grabbing the barrel of the weapon, pulling it away from everyone.

The shotgun blast echoed eerily and then time snapped back into focus. Cops tackled the deputy. The ICE agent grabbed Easy as the injured biker sank to the floor. The man's chest was a bloody mess. Mayhem erupted. I realized that I stood alone. Hardass had immediately rushed to Easy, the other Nightriders converged as well. The women split. The pregnant one, Lainey, and the one who looked like a real biker babe both rushed the dog and little girl. The child clung to the dog, who licked the tears on her cheeks. That's

when I realized what she was crying out.
"*DADDY!*"

Gravedigger

LAINEY SCOOPED NONI into her arms and Ginger had her cell phone to her ear, calling Jonah's school. They would take care of the kids. In moments, they'd disappeared down the hallway. Hardy had immediately gone to Easy. The Russian, too. Russki shoved the ICE agent out of the way. The guy was smart not to protest.

Thank fuck the cops had gone for the deputy. If they hadn't, there would have been a blood bath. As it was, the SWAT team leader was handling damage control with his people, Domino with ours. I was the gawddamned sergeant at arms. I needed to shift and help my brothers. Except Shy stood there. Alone. Eyes wide, her expression an odd combination of panic and calculation. She was going to run.

Her attention was focused once again on the drama surrounding saving Easy's life. He'd been shot before and almost died from it. Fucking Hell Dogs. And now some dumbfuck dickwad of a deputy might have killed him this time. She edged back—an involuntary motion, I think. I padded over, getting between her and the door to the kitchen. She wasn't fucking running away from me. Not until I'd claimed her properly.

She was mine. And she would understand that soon enough. First though, we needed to save Easy and deal with the cops. Hardy and the Russian were splattered with Easy's blood. Sam was also elbow deep. Someone needed to call Doc Carson, get his ass over here before they took Easy to the hospital. I heard the sirens—ambulance. Too late. Hardy and Sam would go with him. They'd deal with the authorities.

I sensed the moment Shy made up her mind to run for it by ducking out through the kitchen. She backed up two steps, whirled, and tripped over me. I was on her in a flash, teeth at her throat. Not hard. Just enough to let her know that she could not get away. Panic overwhelmed the calculation and she stiffened. She would stay here until things settled. Until one of my brothers could return her to my room and I could shift to human.

Then I would claim her.

Shy

I SHOULD HAVE been terrified. This wasn't a dog panting in my face, teeth bared. It was a freaking wolf. A freaking *huge* wolf. Hadn't I dreamed a wolf before, when I was tied up? The animal released my throat but he still straddled me. I didn't move. I'm not an idiot. The chaos around me turned into a tense standoff with the cops on one side, the bikers on the other with the idiot deputy and the wounded man in the middle.

Sirens stopped outside and then three firefighters were hustling through the front entrance. I caught a glimpse of the woman's face as one of the bikers pulled her back. She was so pale I thought she might pass out. It was weird. Her hands and shirt were covered in blood and she'd been right in the thick of things working on the gunshot victim. Then I caught a murmured order from the president.

"Stay with her, Domino. Take her to the children. If the worst happens, they will keep her alive."

What did that mean? That she'd kill herself if her old man died? What the hell was up with that? Especially since they had kids. The biker who'd pretended to be Gravedigger put his arm around the woman to draw her away but she refused, color coming back into her face. Her eyes snapped with anger as she rounded on the man the bikers called The Russian.

"No. I'm going with him. He won't leave as long as I'm there. I won't let him." She was fierce and determined and my heart lurched as my brain churned through the information I'd heard. The Russian guy didn't think she'd kill herself, but that she'd die if her old man did, though the kids might make her want to live. And she thought she could keep her old man alive by sheer will alone. That was...too weird and I didn't know what to think about that.

I pulled my attention back to my predicament and looked up into the eyes of the wolf above me. I knew those eyes. Somehow. But that was crazy. This was a wolf but those eyes... They stared into mine unblinking and I recognized the intelligence in them. And the...possessiveness. His muzzle curled into a snarl as one of the bikers approached us.

"We need to get her out of here, Digger," the biker whispered urgently.

I twisted my head, looking for Gravedigger. I'd heard others call him by the shortened name. He was nowhere to be seen. The wolf growled again, his eyes still on the biker, but he backed away. Before I could react, the man jerked me to my feet and whisked me into the kitchen. The wolf padded in our wake. I managed to catch a glimpse of the man's name. Rebel.

Within moments, we were outside, across the courtyard, and inside the other building. Rebel didn't quite frog-march me but it was close. His hand on my biceps was strong and controlling but also very careful, as if he didn't want to hurt me. The wolf trailed us but when Rebel pushed me into Gravedigger's room, the door slammed behind me and I was alone.

SIXTEEN

Gravedigger

SHIFTING BACK TO human form in Domino's room, I borrowed jeans and boots. I yanked on a T-shirt. My cut was in my room. Where Shy was. Fuck but she tied me up in knots. My wolf had claimed her. Twice. It was time for me to do the same.

I stalked into my room without knocking. She stepped out of the bathroom and froze. The bitter odor of ammonia mixed with rotten eggs wafted between us. Fear and guilt. I wanted to know why. And I wanted her. I looked her up and down, caught a hint of violets and brown sugar. I inhaled, sorting through scents and smiled as a whiff of bourbon and brownies hit my nose. She was getting aroused. About fucking time.

Shy stood her ground as I prowled toward her. Part of me wanted her to run. Okay, the wolf wanted her to run. He wanted to chase her. Catch her. Pounce on her. Put his teeth to the back of her neck and dominate our mate. My dick liked that idea, just so long as we got those damn sweats off her so we could mount and fuck her hard. Her chin came up and her eyes snapped with defiance. The bite of lighter fluid chewed through the brownies. That was okay. I liked that too.

"I thought you were in the hospital." Was she glad I was on my feet?

"Why would you think that?" I couldn't help the sarcasm.

Her gaze flickered and that stubborn chin dropped as her eyes searched my body. Then she fisted her hands and her spine stiffened. "I pretty much gutted you."

"You tried."

Her mouth dropped open and my dick wanted to climb out of the jeans I wore. It wanted to thrust between those moist lips and down her throat. I wanted to suck the tits she stuck out at me as her shoulders straightened. But I really wanted to taste her cunt just to see if it was as sweet as her arousal smelled. I finally looked her in the eye again and they'd gone smoky. Movement drew my attention back to her mouth. Her tongue swiped her bottom lip, leaving it wet. Fuck me.

"Do you have any idea how much I want to fuck you right now?" My voice was more wolf than human, but I didn't give a shit. She inhaled a shuddering breath. I stepped closer. "I want to strip your clothes off, but once you're naked, I can't decide what to do first. I want you kneeling in front of me, your lips around my dick, my hands in your hair, fucking your mouth. I want you flat on your back, knees wide while I eat you out until you scream for me to stick my dick in your pussy.

I want your mouth. Your cunt. Your ass. I'll have all three before we're done."

Shy shuddered again, her eyes going half-lidded. I had her now. I'd fuck her. Claim her. And the world be damned.

Then I caught her scent. Stale beer and puke mixed with cinnamon rolls. If that combination wouldn't put a man off food for a week, nothing would. Good thing I wasn't a man. I understood both her disgust and her desire. For once, my wolf counseled me to slow down, to consider what I was doing. And how I was going about it.

Shy stood with her back pressed against the wall. When had she moved? I'd been so lost in my lust that I hadn't noticed. Fuck. The wolf had, though, and he was pissed that I'd scared our mate. I deep breathed a few times, finding focus and control. I'd heard that getting moonstruck was akin to being slammed by a semi-truck. Fucking truth, that. I needed to back the hell off.

"I'm sorry."

My apology took her off guard. My nose crinkled at the combined scents of blueberries and bleach, which cleared away all the rest. She was confused. Which made sense. Me too. I never apologized to anyone, but she was my mate. I didn't want to scare her. I wanted to fuck her. I wanted to claim her. Hurting her was beyond comprehension, but I realized now that my unfettered lust had done just that. She was prepared for me to rape her.

I realized my fingers were tangled in my

hair as I scrubbed at my head. Like that would help me think or something. It took conscious effort to drop my hands to my sides. We needed to start over, and I had no fucking clue how to make that happen. I backed away until I could lean against the door.

"Will you let me go?" There was only the faintest quiver in her voice, accompanied with the musty, dank smell of an abandoned house. She was resigned to being a prisoner.

"Maybe." My wolf paced, anxious about my answer, then he caught the fragrance of lavender. Shy had a touch of hope now. I was such a fucking bastard because there was no way I—or my wolf—would ever let her go. But maybe we could convince her to stay of her own free will. She wasn't a sweet butt, here strictly for my pleasure. She wasn't a club whore I could use and toss away. She was my mate, the woman I was meant to cherish, the one I would plant my seed in with the hope of bringing my child into this world.

And damn if I didn't sound like a pussy-whipped wimp, all full of romantic bullshit. Yeah. I was well and truly moonstruck. And I didn't give a good gawddamn because eventually, I'd be buried balls deep in her sweet pussy.

"Who are you?" She whispered the question.

How to answer that... It would be easier to explain what I was.

"I'm Gravedigger," I said, as if that explained everything. Maybe it did.

"Who are you really?"

I was tired suddenly and I discovered that I was scrubbing at my face and head again. "I've been Gravedigger since I was eighteen. I'm a Nightrider. I'm the national sergeant at arms."

"You kill people."

She had me there. I had. I would. It's what I did. The answer was so obvious I didn't speak. And that pretty much summed up who I was. I was also a Wolf, and her mate. The unwritten rules said I should tell her. Thing is, I never played by the rules. That's what being part of the outlaw one percent was all about. We lived life the way we wanted and all the rest be damned.

She walked toward me, curiosity in her expression and scent. Ripe bananas. Ugh. Still, I braced as she came closer. I knew she didn't have a weapon but she could still hurt me. My wound wasn't anywhere close to being healed. A well-placed kick or hit would seriously hamper me. She stopped, about three feet away, probably thinking she was far enough to dodge if I went for her. Anywhere in this room wasn't far enough.

She watched me like a curious dog, her head tilted slightly to the side as she attempted to figure me out. "I hate you."

I laughed. Which pissed her off. "Yeah, and?"

"I'm serious."

"Yeah, and?" I lifted one shoulder in a shrug. "Thing is, you need to get over it."

"Get over it?" And just like that, she was in my face. Hers was flushed with anger, eyes narrowed to slits, her lips a thin, bloodless slash.

And just like that, my arms were around her, my mouth covering hers, kissing, teasing until her lips lost the hard and went soft beneath my assault before opening for me. I swept my tongue into her mouth, mating with her tongue. Her heart hammered against my chest. Her quick inhalation pressed her tits against me. I widened my stance, one leg centering between hers. The arm I'd snaked around her back pulled her hips closer so she could ride my thigh.

Damn but I wanted her naked, and me too. What would her slick pussy feel like rubbing across my skin? Her legs clenched around mine and her hips tilted back and forth as she rubbed against me. A little moan escaped into my mouth.

"Strip." My wolf was too close to the surface. I didn't care.

She pushed against me and tore her mouth away. "No."

"Strip, babe."

"I'm not your *babe*."

I should probably tell her that my wolf loved a good fight. It was all part of the hunt. "Then touch yourself."

"No!" Her voice sharp now, she glared at me.

I smiled, reached backed and grabbed the neck of the T-shirt I wore and jerked it over my head. Her eyes blazed but she couldn't help herself. She just had to check me out. I knew the moment her gaze landed on the wicked cut. I hadn't stopped to bandage it. She sucked air and backed away. I followed, not giving her room, until the backs of her legs hit the side of the bed. She went down. I snagged her ankles and yanked the sweats down her legs. The only thing between my hunger and her cunt was a pair of white cotton panties.

"You're wet."

She pushed up on her elbows, ready to deny it until I touched her. Air whistled between her teeth as she gasped. I watched as she flexed her right hand, fingers opening and closing as her eyes fixed on my crotch. I cupped my dick. "You want me."

Her throat worked as she swallowed. Her eyes went unfocused beneath her lowered lashes. "You pick," I offered. "Where do you want me first? And what part?"

The smell of blueberries and bleach was back. I'd confused her. "I'm going to fuck you, babe. I'm going to fuck your mouth, your cunt, and your ass. I don't care in what order. I'm also going to eat you. I'm just letting you pick where we start."

Her chest expanded and I knew I had her for sure. The scent of her arousal wrapped me up in unbreakable chains. She was mine, but she owned me.

🐾 🐾 🐾 🐾

Shy

I SHOULD HAVE said no. I should have pushed him away, demanded that he let me go. I'd come here to kill him. I'd done my damnedest to do so. By rights, I should've been dead since I'd failed to take him out. The MC should have murdered me, stuffed my body in Mitch's truck and sunk it in some lake never to be found. Instead, they...what?

They'd had every intention of hurting me. Why else tie me to that chair in the basement? But then that wolf...dog...animal charged into the room and bit me. Hysterical laughter bubbled inside me, looking for an escape valve. Maybe that thing was a werewolf, and I'd turn furry on the next full moon. I almost laughed because the idea was insane.

I should've said no. Gravedigger had been pretty certain he'd take me. Even against my will. Except that's not what he was doing. He was...seducing me? That made me want to laugh too. Bikers didn't seduce. They took what they wanted. It was up to the woman to get herself off if that's why she was having sex. Except he'd changed the rules on me.

Sex was something to take the edge off. Always had been. I can't say that I was scarred by my childhood. My parents had no boundaries and when they were high and horny, they did it wherever the urge hit, no matter who was there to see. That included Becca and me. The same scenario played out in the various clubhouses where we found ourselves. Becca was careful when she and Bozo were together but that didn't mean the other bikers were. I'd learned to be a mouse, creeping around the edges of the room, eyes down, ears attuned to something other than the squishy sounds of sloppy sex.

Mitch and Kathy were very proper. If they did it at all, it was behind closed doors and without a sound. I remember when Kathy, face flaming and with lots of ums and ahs, explained the "facts of life." Whenever I thought of that phrase, I made mental finger quotes around it. At the time, I nodded dumbly, managed a muffled thank you, and we both fled the encounter.

While living with them, I didn't date. Didn't have boyfriends. That followed me into the army. At the same time, the idea of getting myself off had no real appeal. I had nothing against dick and when I got too wound up, I found a fuck buddy for a one-nighter. That had always worked. Until now.

Chemistry was something that should remain a school subject. Still, people talked about it when it came to two people getting together or getting it on. Movies. Romance novels. Entertainment shows. Love—or lust— at first sight was a myth. Until I met Gravedigger. Looking back, I'd been aware of him the moment he walked into the clubroom not knowing he was the real Gravedigger. And it wasn't just because I was keeping track of all my enemies. Nope, there was an aura around him that turned my insides into melted goo.

And every time I opened my mouth to deny what was between us, I kissed him back.

"You pick," he reminded me, and I had to think. Pick what? Then he dropped to his knees, spread my legs and bent forward. Swallowing, I tensed as his hand tore my panties and found my clit. His thumb pressed against it, rubbing. I looked down my body, found his eyes glued to my face as sensation exploded inside me.

"You're wet."

Of course I was. I wanted this man with an ache so deep I couldn't explain it.

"This," he said, breathing deep before his tongue swiped between my labia, then plunged into my vagina. "Is mine."

Two of his fingers replaced his tongue, curling inside me, working with exquisite slowness, his thumb still rubbing my clit. When he pulled his hand away and held it up for me to see, his fingers glistened. "Open your mouth," he ordered. I did and he plunged his fingers between my lips. I tasted myself and rather than being grossed out, I was…curious.

"Sweet cunt." He all but purred. "Do you want to suck my dick before or after I fuck you?"

I opened my mouth but no words came out. His expression turned predatory as his eyes hooded. His words were crude but they turned me on even more. How was that even possible? The muscles deep inside me were clenching uncontrollably and I knew.

"After," I breathed. I needed him inside me, deep inside, filling me. Making me his. I curled up and stretched out my hand, cupping his dick through his jeans as tension stretched between us and I could smell our desire. My need had become an ache only this man could cure.

Gravedigger's control snapped. He jerked away from my hand, stood and stripped. He was... My breath caught and I licked my lips. He was big and perfect and I wanted him. He caught my shoulders and pulled me to the edge of the bed. One hand gripped my jaw, forcing my mouth open and before I could catch a breath, he plunged his cock between my lips. I choked and he pulled back immediately. That surprised me. He breathed deeply, like he struggled to control himself. His hands tangled in my hair and he fucked my face. Just like he promised.

I tasted his pre-cum. It was thick and rich, salty but with a taste of something...wild. I writhed, my hips rocking because my vagina was empty. I dropped one hand to play with myself, something I'd never done. Gravedigger stopped me with a growl. "Your pussy is mine, Shiane. *Mine*. Nobody, not even you, touches it unless I say so."

And then he was spinning me around and positioning me on my hands and knees. Seconds later, the head of his cock brushed between those other lips before centering at my opening. He thrust hard, filling me in one stroke. He was big and it hurt as my muscles tried to stretch around him. He didn't move and the burn lessened enough I could feel his cock throbbing.

"Fuck, babe." He had to breathe before he had the control to say more. "So fuckin' tight. I knew I'd love this pussy." My center throbbed at his words and I clenched my muscles tight. "Fuuuuck."

He bucked against me, withdrawing only an inch or two before pushing back in. His balls slapped against my mound as he slammed into me, again and again. Faster and faster he moved, his strokes becoming longer and harder and I thought I'd lose my mind. He grunted and growled above me. I whimpered and moaned. This was sex at its rawest. Dirtiest. And I didn't care. Pain and pleasure mixed as I spiraled higher and higher.

Then his cock was gone but fingers plunged into me, curling through my wetness. Before I could protest, his cock was back inside me but those fingers, silky with my desire, teased my rear entrance. I tensed but his other hand found my clit. I bowed my back just as he plunged two fingers into my ass. I screamed. Not because it hurt but because that was exactly what I needed to send me over the edge. My world shattered under a Fourth of July fireworks show.

Gravedigger's arms were suddenly around me, keeping me from collapsing to the bed. His chest pressed to my back as he hunched against me. Even though my inner muscles continued to spasm around him, I felt his cock swell and then throb as he climaxed inside me.

His teeth caught the muscle joining my shoulder with my neck and he growled, "You. Are. Mine." Then he bit down, marking me. I fought for just an instant and then...I didn't understand what happened. Some sense...like a *knowing* settled over me. There was no going back, no do-overs because I belonged to the big, bad biker

SEVENTEEN

Gravedigger

SHY EVENTUALLY WENT back to her apartment. After three days. Three days of her in my bed. Three days of fucking. And talking. We did a little of that. Hell, she'd even wormed my legal name out of me. She'd laughed. "Shane and Shiane. We could be twins," she teased. I shut her up by kissing and then fucking her.

She was my mate. I'd claimed her but she hadn't accepted me. Not really. Her body had. All I had to do was look at her and she went wet for me. Thank fuck. I had her body but I didn't truly have her heart. Or her head. And that sucked donkey balls. My brothers gave me all kinds of shit, except those who'd found their mates. They kept their mouths shut, their eyes knowing. I tossed back a shot of tequila and laughed bitterly. I'd taken everything I ever wanted in my life. Every fucking thing. I even took Shiane without asking, without telling her what my claiming meant, without telling her what the hell I was.

The Russian studied me from across the bar. He was a cold bastard but damn if I wouldn't follow him into the bowels of hell. He was so damn icy, he might just put out the fires down there. Like almost every night, there was a party here at the clubhouse. The sweet butts were strutting their stuff and a few of the old ladies had shown up. Shy didn't wear my colors. Yet. The brothers knew she was off limits because she wore my scent. No outsiders this time so I wasn't too worried. She had to get used to club life because I damn sure wasn't leaving my brothers. Not even for her. She was mine and if she couldn't adapt, I'd keep her separate, which wouldn't sit well with anyone. Especially me and the man currently staring at me.

A sweet butt pressed against my back, rubbing her tits over my patch, her arms circling my waist. I peeled her off none too gently, growling at her. "Don't fucking touch me. I have an old lady."

"So?" she slurred at me, arms snaking around my neck as she tried to kiss me. I pushed her away and she went down on her ass. "So, you don't touch me. Ever." Ignoring her, I poured myself another shot and tossed it back.

"You have to tell her." The Russian continued staring at me.

I knew that. "Yeah? I can't wait until it happens to you, Russki. You'll find out damn fast how easy it isn't."

"Easy. Hard. Does not matter. You must tell her."

"Tell me what?" Shy slid in beside me, her

thigh brushing mine as she hitched a hip on the empty barstool. She batted her lashes at the Russian. "Anybody ever tell you that you're big and scary?"

I saw the wolf flash in his eyes but his lips twitched. Thank fuck he thought she was cute and funny. Me too. She cut her eyes my direction. "In fact, he's even scarier than you, Digger. I didn't figure there was anyone who could surpass your fear quotient."

Swiveling her around on the stool, I pushed her knees apart to make room for me. "Keep being so damn cute and I'll fuck you right here."

Her face flushed and she sputtered at me, but I caught the hint of interest in her expression. She wasn't an exhibitionist and mated brothers were more discreet, but I could tell the idea excited her. In a dark corner, with a crowd not paying attention like the first time I'd gotten my fingers inside her? Fuck yeah. I inhaled and her desire hit me like a freight train.

"Later, babe," I promised.

Shy

HOW DID HE do that to me? One look. One growl. One innuendo and I was hot and ready for him. It was like part of him lived inside me, like I could picture whatever he was thinking in those moments. When I walked through the door and saw that skank all over him, I'd been ready to nail him to the nearest wall. Then I watched him basically ignore her, and when she hit the floor butt first, I wanted to cheer. That chick was not part of the sisterhood so I didn't feel too bad.

With him standing close, touching me, something inside me unwound. I'd been tense since going back to the garage apartment. Mitch and Kathy didn't say anything, but I knew they were disappointed in me. I promised myself to break it off with Gravedigger. That lasted all of a day. By midnight that first day apart, I was a basket case. I'd grabbed my bike and was pedaling down the driveway when a dark shadow stepped into my path. Gravedigger. I stashed my mountain bike in the bushes lining the drive and followed him to his motorcycle.

I felt like a teenager, sneaking out and then sneaking back in past curfew. I'd made Digger bring me home just before dawn, stopping before we were close enough to the house that his Harley pipes would wake Mitch. Day two didn't get any easier. What was it about this man? He'd gotten under my skin, worse than an itch I couldn't scratch. He was an addiction. I was only happy when he was there, close.

I leaned in, ready to steal a kiss he was ready to give me. Then I was flying sideways. Since I wasn't drunk, I landed balanced and ready to defend myself. A woman about my age glowered at me. One of the sweet butts, if

I had to guess.

"Stay away from my old man." She was all but spitting.

"I don't see a property patch on your skanky ass."

"I'll have his sooner than later. He's mine." Her hand, tipped with long, red nails flashed out. Her slap caught me flat-footed. Cat fighting wasn't my thing.

"Not hardly," I replied calmly and then decked her with a right jab. She went down in a heap. It all happened so fast, only a few people noticed.

Digger stared at me, something red and feral sparking in the depths of his eyes. "I want to fuck you."

That made me laugh. "Of course you do." Of course, I wanted to fuck him right back. "Let's go to your room."

He reached for me but before I could take his hand, a man pushed in behind me. His fingers closed over my biceps as he jerked me around to face him.

"This the little bitch you didn't kill, Gravedigger?" The guy's breath smelled like roadkill and his pupils were the size of pinpricks. I didn't know what drug he was on but the guy was flying on rage and stupidity. I sensed both Digger and the man they all called the Russian stiffening.

"Why are you here, Snake?"

The hair on my arms prickled and my hind brain wanted to run and hide. I'd never heard any man's voice contain so much menace.

"Ya fucked up, Gravedigger. Betrayed the brotherhood." He stabbed his finger toward a spot across the room.

I reluctantly followed the direction he was pointing only to see the wolf skin nailed to the wall. I'd been curious about that, guessing it had something to do with the leaping wolf that was part of the Nightrider patch.

"Brick was our president and you disobeyed him. And then—" The idiot stabbed his finger toward the Russian. "You brought this motherfucker in to do your dirty work."

Digger stopped breathing, his body so hard it felt like a brick wall at my back.

"Fuck you. Both of you."

I caught the barest glance the Russian and Gravedigger exchanged before I realized that we were ringed in by a group of Nightriders. I'd met a few of them. Easy. Hollywood. Radar. Domino. Another guy was there, one I'd seen around but hadn't met. His vest had a patch with the name "Gunner" on it. His expression reminded me of both the Russian and Gravedigger. There was absolutely no emotion there.

That's when I realized the room was quiet. No music. No talking. Some of the brothers were hustling the women out through the front entrance. The only women they ignored where those wearing property patches. Old ladies. I hadn't noticed them when I walked in. I'd only seen that club bitch climbing all over my man.

I stopped breathing for a moment. My man? Digger told me he'd claimed me, that I was his. I'd brushed him off, despite the feeling that swamped me after our first time together. But if I'd had claws in that moment, I would have unleashed them and gone for the woman's face. I might be his, but he was mine too. As soon as I admitted it, another of the coiled places inside me relaxed. It didn't matter that he was a biker. A Nightrider. It only mattered that he was mine, and I was his.

His arm circled around my chest, pulling me back against him. I relaxed into his hold and it was like he knew. I felt something uncoil in him too.

"You go too far, Snake," the Russian was saying. He didn't sound particularly threatening, but I watched the faces around me go blank. My cop senses went on high alert. Basking in the glow of all things sexy and yummy about Digger, I'd forgotten the bottom line—he was a criminal. The biker known as Snake was a dead man. I'd bet everything I owned on that fact. Then I caught the Russian staring at me. Was I about to bet my life?

Gravedigger

I WATCHED SHY pace the room, front to back, side to side, and stayed out of her way.

At the moment, I was pretty damn sure she was pissed as hell and probably hated my guts. She stopped directly under the wolf skin, her face flushed with anger, chest heaving, fists clenched. Gunner and Easy had marched Snake into church while I locked Shy in my room. Now we were back in the clubhouse, church over.

Turned out old Snake had nursed a grudge ever since the Russian challenged and killed Brick. And he'd held a grudge against me personally from the moment Brick made me an enforcer, which he'd essentially done the night we raided the Death Hawgs. Snake was currently down in the pit thinking about his sins. He'd spewed some interesting shit once the Russian started his particular brand of questioning. We'd finish dealing with the bastard eventually. Currently, I had to deal with my woman. Too bad half the club was watching.

Despite the audience, it was time she faced the facts. "You're mine."

"I'd be better off dead."

Too bad that was all too easily arranged, which was the whole point for her being here. Well, that and there was no way I'd let her walk away from me.

Shy stared up at me, eyes glinting under the cheap pool table light. "Why didn't you kill me? Back then."

Fuck. I rubbed the back of my neck, stalling while I figured out what to say. "I don't kill babies." Hell, she'd been a kid, but she'd looked like a baby, huddled there over that girl's body.

"You killed my sister."

I hadn't, exactly, but someone had. We normally tried to avoid collateral damage. That included kids and old ladies. "That was business."

"So, what's this?"

Technically, this was business too. Seemed ol' Snake had been parlaying with the Hell Dogs and according to him, those bastards wanted her. Dead or alive. The Nightriders wanted her alive. *I* wanted her alive. My wolf clawed at my guts, driven to protect her, especially from me. I had so fucking much blood on my hands I was completely whacked to think I could touch her, that she'd ever want me to. Even though the wolf and I had marked her and claimed her as our mate. For three fucking days. My balls had almost exploded from that claiming.

"Am I just business, Gravedigger?"

The name "Shy" didn't fit this fierce warrior woman. "You're way more than business, darlin'. I'd die to protect you."

"If I don't kill you first, *darlin'*." Her lip curled into a snarl and I fought the urge to kiss her. She'd probably claw my eyes out, but the idea of her clawing my skin as I drove into her hot, slick pussy? Oh fuck yeah. I was one sick puppy.

I grinned, unable to stop myself because yeah...sick puppy. Then I watched her shoulders slump and it was like someone let the air out of one of those stupid pool floaty things. Caught in her liquid gaze, I sobered.

"I couldn't even say goodbye. There was no body to bury. She was my only family and you took her from me."

She had me there. Unable to stay away, I stalked her and once I caught her, I cupped her face in my hands, my thumbs automatically brushing away the tears she had no clue she was shedding.

"It wasn't us, baby girl," I whispered. She tensed, remembering that I'd called her that before. "We didn't kill your sister." Her mouth curled into a sneer but I kissed her before she could lash out. Pulling back so she could see my eyes, so I could see hers, I told her the truth. All of it.

"The Death Hawgs. They were stupid. Kids for the most part playing bad asses. When we hit the house, they opened fire. Indiscriminately. When I checked you out later, I was surprised as hell that you hadn't been hit. Your sister took a forty-five bullet through the chest. We use nine millimeters. Always have."

"How do you know?"

"I dug the bullet out of her. Out of all the bodies. We only took down two Hawgs, Shy. Only two. All the rest were hit by friendly fire."

"You're lying."

"No, baby girl. I'm not."

"I saw you. You had a pistol in your hand."

"Yeah. I was carrying. But the Hawgs

were drunk and high. They weren't expecting us. And we didn't go in there to kill. Beat the crap out of, send them back to Tennessee with their tails between their legs, yeah. And we didn't know you or your sister would be there."

"I don't believe you."

I shrugged. "Believe what you want, Shy, but I'm telling you truth."

"But the man, the one called Brick, he told you to bury me." There was no heat in her voice, only dull acceptance.

"No." I did lie then. Brick meant for me to dispose of the child Shy had been. His callous disregard was one of many reasons his hide now decorated the wall behind Shy. "He told me to bury *this*. That meant the scene, the bodies."

"But...I saw. I was a witness. I could have—"

"But you didn't," I cut her off. "Yeah, you were traumatized. Yeah, you heard names, but there was nothing to tie us to what happened except the words of a scared kid."

"Where is she?"

Her abrupt change of subject caught me off guard. "Who, babe?"

"Becca. My sister. What did you do with her?"

"She's gone, Shiane."

Her eyes came to mine at last. It was the finality in my voice. "She was my sister." Her voice was the barest whisper and it cracked on the last word. My heart cracked too. When her fist swung at my face, I didn't duck. I accepted the punch. And her anger. I deserved it. She went crazy then, pounding my chest with her fists. I absorbed every blow.

When Easy made to move, I shook my head and shot him a look that ordered him to back off. He did, with reluctance. I couldn't blame him. I was still healing but I had to do this for Shy. For my mate. She'd held on to this hurt for fifteen years. It was time for her to let it go.

Twenty brothers stood around, watching. The Russian frowned, unhappy. That was bad. Hell, this whole fucking mess was bad. I'd never been able to shake the memory of that night, of the little girl who smelled of rusted iron, violets and brown sugar. My wolf pawed at my insides. He'd known all along. Shiane Roarke belonged to us. She was ours to claim, to protect. Fate was a bitch because there was no way this woman would ever let me love her. We'd deal with it. She was my mate. That's just the way it was.

EIGHTEEN

Shy

I'D BEEN UPSET when Digger dumped me in his room and locked the door behind him. Then I'd been scared. He'd lifted my phone so I couldn't even call 9-1-1. Not that I would. That Snake guy was a nasty piece of work, and I figured he'd get what he deserved. Deep down, I'd always been a realist and something of a fatalist as well. I wasn't above turning into a vigilante and basically? That's what club culture was about. A rival club messed with your club? You retaliated. MCs were very Old Testament about the whole justice/punishment thing.

After leaving me alone for most of the night, Gravedigger reappeared and walked me back over to the clubhouse. Where he'd declared I was his in front of his brothers. I was tired. Scared. Emotionally bruised. And I was furious. So, I lost it. Now, my hands hurt from beating on Digger. He'd just stood there, absorbing every blow I landed. His expression never changed. But his eyes. God, his eyes. The sorrow I saw in them... My heart twisted.

"You're still mine, babe."

The hell I was! I suddenly didn't care what he was feeling. I wanted to hurt him like he'd hurt me. My brain disengaged and my mouth took over.

"The only thing we have going for us is hot sex."

He gave me a slow grin guaranteed to melt my panties—if I'd been wearing any. Like an idiot, I'd come prepared for his brand of fun and I was tired of ripped underwear—especially my nice stuff. Lingerie wasn't cheap.

"And that's a bad thing?"

"Are you sure you want to do this here? In front of your *brothers*?" I spit out the last word, coating it with as much sarcasm as I could muster.

I stood my ground, defiant, waiting for his comeback. He was surrounded by his brothers and I was all alone. The old ladies had congregated in a small gaggle clear across the room. Not that I wanted or needed their back-up. This was between him and me, and if he didn't have the balls to go private with this fight, we'd duke it out right here in front of God and everyone. I was past caring. Losing control felt freaking good.

Digger tilted his head, watching but he didn't speak. Neither did anyone else. In fact, no one moved. They might have been playing that kid's game where the players freeze in place until the person who's it turns around and then they'd try to sneak up on whoever was "It." Statues? Something like that.

I didn't take my eyes off Gravedigger. His face showed not a trace of emotion. I didn't have time to react as his hand lashed out and fastened on my arm. He reeled me to him and then we were turning and moving. Somebody inhaled quickly. I thought it was one of the old ladies, but Digger was dragging me along in his wake so fast I didn't have time to check before we were outside and headed back to his room.

He shoved me through the door, followed me in, and slammed it behind us. I whirled to confront him. His face hadn't changed. It could have been carved from granite for all the expression on it. Leaning back against the door, he crossed his arms over his chest and only then did a flicker of emotion appear in his eyes. Smug bastard.

"So, sex is a bad thing?" He was quick to remind me where we'd left off.

"Between us? Damn straight it is."

His mouth quirked, like he was trying not to laugh. "I thought sex between us was pretty damn good."

Asshole. My temper erupted. I opened my mouth and all sorts of shit spewed out. "I hate you and everything you stand for." My voice didn't waver and rang with my conviction. Points to me. I wasn't my body. I had a brain, even if I wasn't currently using it. And I had a heart. Despite the fantastic sex and the whole asshole alpha male *you're mine* shit, he didn't love me and dammit, I deserved to be loved by the right man. Digger was the wrong man on so many levels I needed an elevator to reach them all.

He didn't move, except to smirk. Fine. I might as well get it all out. "You can turn me on, using my hormones against me, but every time you touch me, I cringe. You represent every bad thing that's ever happened to me. There is nothing between us. Nothing. You kidnapped me. You threatened me. You raped me the first time we were together."

He jerked like I'd slapped him. "Take that back," he growled.

"No." I spat my denial at him.

"I asked you." His voice vibrated with anger. "Repeatedly. You never fucking once said no to me, Shiane. Not one fucking time. I can get pussy any time I fucking want. Yours isn't cut from diamonds. I don't rape women. I didn't rape you." His hands clenched at his sides as he took a step toward me.

Technically, he was correct. He had asked me. Told me, in fact. *Say no*, he'd said. *If you don't want this, want us, tell me now and I'll walk away.* His words echoed in my head. I'd wanted to say no. I'd wanted to leave. But I didn't. I didn't say no and I sure as hell didn't leave or ask him to walk away. I'd wanted him so much my whole body ached.

I lifted my chin. "You're right. I didn't say no, so I guess technically, it wasn't rape. I hate you, Shane *Gravedigger* Cole. I hate your damn motorcycle club. I hate your touch. I hate the way you make my body feel, hate that you make me want you when I want nothing to do with you. You're a criminal. And a bastard. Hear me now. No more. I don't want you to ever touch me again."

The cockiness melted from his expression, to be replaced by...something, some emotion I didn't recognize, not at first. Disappointment? No, something deeper, more...profound. Misery. And anguish. My heart thudded in my chest as he backed away without a word. I'd expected a fight, or more swagger, especially given the cocky smirk he'd worn just a few minutes ago. A fleeting look of sorrow flashed in his eyes and then he was gone, the door clicking to a quiet close behind him.

What the...? Stunned, I stood there, arms wrapped around myself, staring at the door. It wasn't like him to just walk away without a fight. I tiptoed to the door and listened. Nothing. The hallway was dead silent. I tried the doorknob. It turned easily in my hand. That was a first.

Without understanding why, I stepped back into Gravedigger's room and shut the door. My heart thudded against my rib cage so hard I couldn't breathe. I had to lean against the wall. My knees gave out and I slid down until my butt hit the floor, knees bent. What was wrong with me? I felt...devastated. And alone. Did Gravedigger feel this lonely? God, but it hurt. And then there was...nothing. Nothing but blank emptiness. I swiped at tears I was only just then realizing I shed. This is what I wanted, right? To be done with him. To be free.

But who knew freedom would hurt so much?

NINETEEN

Shy

I DON'T KNOW how long I sat there, leaning
back against the wall, before I heard the timid
knock. I rolled to my feet. I caught some
whispers from the other side as I opened the
door and discovered two women standing
there. Both wore leather vests. Old ladies. I
was so miserable I didn't pay them much
attention beyond noticing one was blonde and
the other sported long red hair.

The blonde looked me up and down.
"Shiane, right?"

I partially lifted one shoulder in response.
Anything else seemed like too much effort.

"I'm your ride home. Let's go." She turned
on her heel and strode down the hallway
toward the Barracks' front entrance. The back
of her vest read "Property of Easy." She looked
vaguely familiar but I was so lost in my own
misery, I couldn't place her. The other woman
waited just outside the door. She looked both
older and harder than the blonde.

"What's that make you?" I muttered. "My
bodyguard?"

"Not hardly. Move it."

I stepped out and she gave me a bit of a

shove. Yeah, these two wouldn't ever be my BFFs. Once I cleared the doorway, she shut the door to Gravedigger's room and used a key to lock it. I didn't get a look at her vest so I had no clue who she belonged to. Easy's woman was waiting at the front entrance, door propped open by her hip. She nodded toward a tricked-out Jeep Wrangler. I looked all over the courtyard. No Gravedigger. No Gravedigger's Harley. I considered making a break for the clubhouse to see if he was there.

The women followed me, a step behind. As if she could read my mind, the blonde ordered, "Don't even think about it." She had a good command voice. Mine was better. "Just get in the Jeep. If you don't, some of the guys will move your sorry ass outside the gate and you can frickin' walk home."

Huh. An MC old lady who didn't cuss. Except the redhead was snickering. "Is Noni still playing mockingbird?"

And things fell into focus with a thunderclap. This was the woman whose little girl was in the middle of that raid, whose old man had been shot. Crap. But... I stopped dead and the redhead bumped into me.

"What the hell?" she yelled.

I whirled, stabbed a finger at the blonde. "You're Easy's old lady." She gave me a *d'uh* look. "He was shot in the chest." Another *d'uh*. "I saw him tonight. Standing there in the clubhouse. Laughing and drinking and..." She exchanged a look with the redhead. "How is that even possible?"

Had that whole thing been a set-up? It wasn't possible. I knew that dumb-ass deputy and he hated bikers. When Mitch was still on the force, he complained about the guy all the time. I cut my gaze back and forth between the two women.

"Get in the damn car or walk." The blonde's voice was so cold it felt like her words cut my skin.

I got in the damn car.

Shy

A WEEK. I'd turned into a basket case within forty-eight hours. I lay awake at night, the windows open, listening for the sound of Harley pipes—a sound that never came. Mitch had left some applications for me. Lee's Summit PD. Some from neighboring towns, a couple of the local counties. His not-so-subtle hint that I should get a job and since I was military trained to be a cop, I should be a cop. I shied away from that commitment. First, it was a commitment. Second, there were moments when I wanted to kill Digger for what he was putting me through, especially right after I considered crawling into the clubhouse on my hands and knees to beg him to take me back. Murder could be a career killer for a cop.

I was sitting on the deck watching the sun go down when I heard the back door open and close. A minute later, a light tread sounded from the stairs. Kathy. Shit. I pasted a pleasant expression on my face. She came bearing a plate of cookies. Bless her. She still thought of me as that traumatized ten-year-old. Sadly, she wasn't too far off the mark at the moment.

"Hey, sweetie. I made a big batch of these. Your favorite." She held the plate out. I accepted it, snagged a double-chocolate chunk and pecan cookie, and set the plate on the little side table. Kathy settled into the other deck chair, her worried eyes studying me.

"Don't start," I mumbled around the bite of cookie in my mouth.

"We care, honey."

"I know, Kathy. There's just…stuff going on."

"You know if you ever need or want to talk—"

"Yeah." I cut her off. They'd never had kids and they'd done their best to make me believe I was theirs. They loved me despite my best efforts. I reached over and patted her arm. "Nothing to talk about, Kathy. I'm fine. Promise."

She sighed, then settled back against the cushions. This had always been her ploy, thinking she could wait me out. I'd been a sullen teen. Now I was a sullen adult. Something rustled in the bushes down below and Kathy sat forward, peering intently at a dark shadow among the plants in her garden.

"Someone around here has a big, black

German Shepherd and he keeps getting out."

Wait. What? I pushed out of my chair and casually strolled to the deck railing. Hitching my hip on the top bar, I watched out of the corner of my eye. Movement flickered but I didn't get a good look. Kathy started to speak but I gestured at her to stay quiet. I leaned down and snagged another cookie, making a show of eating it. If the dog was a stray, maybe it would come out to check for a food source. We didn't have to wait long. A black nose appeared between two small evergreens, then a black muzzle, a head, and a large body.

I almost fell over backwards, which would have hurt when I bounced off the ground a story below. The animal cocked its head, watching me as intently as I watched it. I knew this animal. Him. This was the fourth time I'd seen him—three times at the Nightrider clubhouse and now here. At least, I thought it was the same dog. Only I didn't think it was a dog. Wolf. I was pretty sure of that. Which made some weird sense given that the Nightrider patch featured a wolf.

The dang thing just stood there, staring at me. Like he was waiting for me to say something. Or do something. Kathy appeared next to me. In the barest whisper, she said, "That is *not* a dog."

I figured she'd know, given she volunteered at the animal shelter all the time. "I think it might be a wolf or a hybrid," I whispered back.

"Wolf," Kathy stated, certain. "He's

magnificent."

He was. Black as night with golden eyes ringed in forest green. And he was watching Kathy and me—especially me. He looked hungry and I had the distinct feeling that if I'd been alone, he would have decided I'd make a good dinner. He tilted his head, the gesture and the expression on his face almost...human. And that was just crazy. Even though I'd thought the same thing when I'd seen him the first time in the basement of the Nightrider clubhouse. When he'd charged in like he was trying to save me. My hand automatically went to my shoulder where his teeth had marked me. I closed my eyes and shook the weirdness out of my head.

"Oh," Kathy breathed. "He's gone. Just like that."

I searched the yard but it was empty. Just like I felt.

Gravedigger

HARDY SPRAWLED on the ground, his back braced against a broad tree trunk. He stared into the underbrush, his gaze fixed on me. "It's time, Digger. You need to come back now. No more of this hide and seek shit."

His voice was low, with a hint of alpha command in it. Not that it would work on me. We'd never tested who was the stronger wolf but I was damn sure he couldn't force me to change. Only the Russian was capable of that.

"I brought your clothes, bro. It's been over a week."

I sank down on my haunches, regarding him unblinkingly, a snarl on my muzzle.

"You don't scare me, Dig. You forget. I work for the Russian, too, plus I served under Mac McIntire. You're tough. But you ain't either of them."

True.

"And not to sound humble, but I can take you."

I snorted, which came out more of a sneeze. Like hell.

"I need to check your wound. I suspect you haven't been shifting nor have you smeared any of the antibiotic ointment on it. That means you've been licking it. We heal fast but that was a wicked wound and wolf spit won't do squat."

I growled, even though he was right. That's exactly what I'd done. If it worked for our wild kin, why wouldn't it work for us?

"I was long gone by the time Brick recruited you." Hardy continued to talk. I growled again. "You were what? Eighteen when that raid happened?" He left on leg stretched out while crooking the other knee to use as a prop for his arm. "Brick didn't have time for his own kid so he damn sure didn't have time for any child that wasn't his. Weird that. Seein' as most of us are hardwired to protect pups."

His head *thunked* back against the tree

and he stared up through the branches to the night sky above. "Once upon a time there was another little girl. Much younger than your Shy. I was thirteen, barely past my first couple of changes. She was in a bad place but she saw me in wolf form and thought I was a lost dog. She would sneak food to me and left an old bowl out, filling it with fresh water every day. I knew she was mine. I don't know how. I just did. But I was thirteen and she was maybe four."

I didn't want to hear this but to get him to shut up, I'd have to change and I wasn't ready for that. I should've just run back into the woods and stayed away. The problem with that, we were Wolves and we were pack animals. Lone Wolves didn't do well. The MC depended on me. I had a place in the hierarchy. *My* place. I growled and stretched out, listening because it suddenly occurred to me that not many Nightriders were left who knew Hardy's story.

"Brick caught me. Went apeshit when he found out her folks were drug addicts and had some tie to the Hell Dogs. Even back then they were our enemies. He called child protective services. Anonymously. Not to protect the kid. To punish me. She cried when they took her away. Not for her parents. For me. Brick made sure I was there to see it."

Fuck. I shifted. Hardy heard my bones popping and stopped talking, thank Christ. When I walked out of the trees, he tossed a bundle of clothes to me. I dressed but Hardy didn't say anything else. The bastard was going to make me ask.

"What happened?"

"Huh?"

"The little girl." My voice cracked from not using it.

Hardy shrugged. "No clue. I haven't seen her since that day. But I learned something."

He stared at the sky again, not speaking. I finished dressing and sat down to pull on my motorcycle boots. Hardy still hadn't said anything else. Asshole. He was doing it on purpose. Then I caught a faint scent. Magnolias. I really looked at the man known as Hardass. He wore an aura of sadness like a quilt. I knew then how he got his road name—not because he was a hardass, but because he had a soft heart. I hunkered down beside him.

"She wasn't really mine, no matter how much I wanted her to be," Hardy murmured. Louder, he added, "You wouldn't have known, Dig. Not back then. No way."

"Then why did I save her?"

"Because you weren't a homicidal fuck like Brick."

That startled a laugh out of me. "Good to know."

TWENTY

Shy

I BREATHED SHALLOWLY and lay still. It was hard since my heart wanted to climb out of my throat and run the hell away. Fight or flight is base instinct and resisting both was harder than anything I'd faced in Afghanistan. Or at the Nightriders' clubhouse.

What had happened? My brain didn't want to come on-line. I remembered. Sort of. Had somebody clobbered me on the back of the head? Gravedigger? The Nightriders? I heard people moving around and it took all my control to stay still. I opened one eye experimentally, couldn't see a thing. I fought off a stab of panic. I'd been hooded, that was all. I did a quick assessment that would have made my SERE trainers proud. My wrists were secured in front of me with plastic ties and my ankles remained free.

Someone stopped next to me. I focused on looking like I was still unconscious. I heard what sounded like a long, indrawn breath sucked in through the nose.

"This one's mine." The growling male voice was filled with...greed. Possessiveness.

And satisfaction. "She smells of the Gravedigger." And now he sounded…amused. "Wakey-wakey, little mouse."

The hood was ripped off my head, and I blinked up at the man peering down at me. Evil radiated from him. "I think, once I tire of you in my bed, I'll send you back to him one piece at a time."

I stopped breathing, and I swear my heart didn't beat as my whole body froze in fear. This man meant every word. Two more men moved in and a needle was jabbed in my neck. I don't know what crap they injected me with but within seconds I had no control over my body. Blessed darkness clouded my vision, and I sank into the oblivion it promised.

🐾 🐾 🐾 🐾

Gravedigger

I WALKED INTO the clubhouse, Hardy at my back, ready to face the Russian. I'd abdicated my position because of a damn woman. So what if she was my mate? I cut and ran, went fucking feral, for chrissakes. Ready to take whatever punishment the Russian dished out, I wasn't prepared for the frigid wall of anger I walked smack-dab into. Shit.

At this rate, I'd be sentenced to a year of being the main attraction at Nightshades, the BDSM club the MC owned. The Russian had certain talents and when he decided to show them off, the club was standing room only.

More than one of us had served as his sub when we were being punished for club infractions. As Wolves, we could take the harsh treatment and recover.

A wave of terror crashed over me and I almost went to my knees. What the fuck? I tasted an imaginary hint of violets and brown sugar on the back of my tongue and then my wolf was clawing his way out of my skin. Feral didn't even come close to describing my animal side.

"What?" I growled out between lengthening canines, my face already elongating into my wolf's muzzle.

"You will stay human, Gravedigger." The Russian's voice was quiet, almost soft even, but it cracked through the air like a bull whip.

My wolf receded just enough for me to reverse the change. I held onto my humanity with bloody claws. "Shianne."

I felt Hardy, Easy, and Domino at my back. Gunner and Radar stood next to the Russian. If they'd hurt her, I'd go down fighting. Radar stepped forward, a laptop in his hands.

"I will lock you down if necessary, Gravedigger, but you need to see this, need to tell us if she is complicit or victim." The Russian held my attention.

Radar set the computer on the bar, waiting for me to approach before keying up the video frozen on the screen. I forced myself to watch as Hell Dogs surrounded Shianne. As they pawed her, kicked her, marked her the way male dogs mark their fucking territory, she made no move to protect herself.

"Run it back," I ordered Radar. "Forward." The scene unfolded again. This time, I ignored the men and focused on Shy's face. No expression. Her face was slack. I studied her eyes. They were unfocused, open but no one was home. "They fucking drugged her."

I always thought anger was a hot emotion—scorching and fierce. But as I clamped down mine with iron-fisted will, I understood the arctic chill I'd felt the moment I walked into the clubhouse. I was going to kill every single one of those motherfuckers. Right after I ripped off their dicks and stuffed them down their throats.

A man walked into the room, but he stayed in the shadows. "Enough," he said. "Send the video." Following a long moment of silence, he stepped into the light. "We'll play with her later, after we've killed the Nightriders." He turned to face what was probably a cell phone set to record video. "You Nightriders have the unfortunate penchant for losing your women to the Hell Dogs."

"Fallen Angel." The name was lost in the snarl of my wolf as he clawed to get out. Didn't matter. The name swelled as it was repeated by every one of my brothers.

I looked at Russki as he reminded me, "She tried to kill you."

"Doesn't fucking matter. She's mine."

The Russian smiled, if you could call the slashing upward tilt of his lips that. "Then we ride."

🐾 🐾 🐾 🐾

Shy

I DIDN'T WANT to open my eyes. Bright light penetrated my closed lids with a throbbing red matching the pounding ache in my head. Not the first time since being dragged into Gravedigger's world that I'd awakened in this predicament. My memory was slowly coming back. At least I wasn't terrified this time. Nope. I was pissed as hell. I'd stopped to fill Mitch's truck with gas and I saw a woman I thought I recognized.

We'd been at the clubhouse, Digger and me. A party. This one came at me all red nails and black mascara claiming I'd stolen Digger from her. She slapped me, hoping for a cat fight. I decked her with a right jab. I don't fight like a girl. That should have ended things. Only it didn't, evidently, because she stood there glaring at me. I topped off the tank, put the nozzle back in the pump, and turned to get into the truck. I remembered her coming up behind me, crashing pain in my head. And then...waking up briefly before they shot me full of something. Now I was awake again.

"Payback's a bitch, girlfriend." I recognized that voice and almost laughed at the sarcasm.

I sensed the woman stood front of me,

leaning over. Time to deal. "Yeah?" Without opening my eyes to see, I kicked out with both feet. One caught her in the gut, the other under the chin. I couldn't have aimed better if I'd tried. She went down in a heap, crying and moaning. I opened my eyes at the sound of slow clapping. The man standing next to me dried the spit in my mouth, as did his colors. Hell Dog. I was staring Death in the face.

"They call me Fallen Angel."

I was so screwed. Terrified. Angry. This was all Digger's fault. Somehow. By dragging me into his world, he'd exposed me to this...monster. I'd looked into the eyes of Taliban fighters who had more compassion than this man.

"You're a Hell Dog." My voice came out flat, unemotional. Good. Taking out the bitch who clobbered me got my blood running. Now that the drugs were out of my system, I was not going to sit back and let these bastards hurt me without a fight.

"No. I am *the* Hell Dog."

Of course, he was. The president. He was as scary as the Russian. Maybe even more. Because this man? He was a complete psychopath. I didn't have many cards to play, so I cashed in all my chips with my next statement.

"My father was a Hell Dog."

Fallen Angel's expression didn't change though his eyes raked over me with hungry greed. I threw up a little in my mouth, knowing instinctively what he had planned for me. I wouldn't go down easy, and this man was just arrogant enough to think he could overwhelm me with his size and muscles. Let him underestimate me.

"Yet you were raised by a cop."

Dang. How did he know that? I refused to drop my eyes, meeting his gaze head-on. "After the Nightriders killed my sister and her old man."

If I could get him to believe that I was only with Gravedigger to get revenge. Which had been true, once. Now? Now I didn't know how I felt, only that if he walked through that door and survived, I'd kiss him and never let him go. He was mine. Just like I was his. Even when I was totally pissed at him.

Something stirred in the shadows of my mind, like a tiny door opening just a crack. *I will find you.*

Only clamping down on my emotions with a strength I'd never needed before kept me from reacting. Gravedigger's voice. In my freaking head. Unnerved, I fought to keep my facade in place.

"So, you *aren't* Gravedigger's whore?"

I spat at him though he stood far enough away the spittle landed harmlessly on the floor. "I'm no man's whore."

"Yet his scent is all over you." A very creepy grin splattered on his face and his eyes crinkled. "Or was until my men marked you."

So far, I'd ignored my damp clothes and the scent of urine. I was just happy I had clothes *on*. It would have been far more demoralizing to strip me naked, not that I was going to put that thought in the bastard's head. Nope. I was pretty damn sure he planned to strip and rape me before the night was over. Or day. I had no clue what time it was, or how long I'd been gone. Would Mitch be looking for me? Could I use his retired cop status as leverage?

"Yeah, real classy of them." I curled my lip in disdain.

The man laughed. And every drop of blood in my body froze. I'd never been so terrified in my life. Not the night Becca was murdered. Not sitting there on that bench covered in my sister's blood. Not standing in the room with a Taliban fighter describing how he would burn me alive after he and all his fellow *warriors* raped every orifice in my body. Not even when I plunged a knife into Gravedigger's back and knew without a doubt that I'd killed both of us.

As his laughter faded away, Fallen Angel inhaled deeply. Eyes the color of smoke fixed on me. "Take her back to her cell. We have things to do before I can indulge myself."

Hands grabbed me and hauled me to my feet. I didn't fight as they hustled me out of the room. Time away from him, time alone in a room would give me the chance to plan my escape. Because I would escape—one way or another. I'd kill myself before I let that man touch me.

Hours might have passed, or minutes. I was alone in the dark. I'd traced the confines of the room with both my feet and hands. The ceiling was low—I could touch it if I jumped. The walls were concrete blocks and there was no window. I found the light—a bare bulb swinging away when my fingers bumped it. There was no string to pull, nor could I find a switch plate on the wall. The door was made of metal, but I got the impression it was a simple industrial grade interior door. Nothing I could break through but not solid. There was also no furniture, nothing from which to fashion a weapon but for the light bulb. I'd have to rely on my hands and feet, and my close-quarters combat training.

I was about to snap the plastic tie holding my wrists together, using a technique taught in SERE school, when I caught a faint sound outside the door. I backed into the farthest corner and squinted my eyes. I didn't want to be blinded if the door opened to bright light, or some idiot shined a flashlight in my eyes. The door opened and Fallen Angel stood there.

He gestured for me to come to him. I didn't move. Wordlessly, he gestured again and I imagined I could feel the mental compulsion he aimed my direction. I stiffened my spine and waited. It didn't take long. Three strides and he was across the room. His grip on my biceps would leave bruises and he lifted me by that one hand so that I was on my tiptoes. Hard to drag my feet when I was mincing across the floor like a ballerina.

The monster hustled me into a hallway

and then into an open space. I finally figured out where I was—an abandoned building that once housed a big-box building supply store.

It came gently at first, the faint vibration through the concrete floor. Then the low rumble of sound, like thunder on the far horizon. Just like that night in Springfield, when I hid in the weeds and watched the massed fury of the Nightriders ride past me in formation.

And then I felt him in my heart. Gravedigger. Was he here for rescue? Or... revenge?

TWENTY-ONE

Gravedigger

WE HAD A network of informants spread all over the KC environs. They didn't take long to locate and spill where the Hell Dogs had taken Shy. The security camera footage from the convenience store where she'd been kidnapped pinpointed her attackers—the club whore who'd come on to me and three Hell Dogs. They'd all die, if not at my hands then the hands of my brothers. My first priority was Shy.

Only twenty of us rode, with more en route as backup from the Kansas side of the state line. Sooner, now than later, the entire club—nationwide—would ride and hunt, taking out every last remaining Hell Dog. If anything happened to Shy, it would be tomorrow, even if I hunted alone.

By the time we rode up to the abandoned warehouse store, our brothers from Kansas were right behind us. The Russian activated everyone as soon as he'd seen the video and Fallen Angel's challenge. I'd hunt my quarry better on four feet. Stripping down, I shifted, muscles and joints stretching and popping in an ecstatic burst of agony. Then I was wolf and I had the stench of prey filling my lungs with each breath.

Shy

THE MONSTER DIDN'T seem to be in a hurry though he kept us moving in the same inexorable way that molten lava flows along eating everything in its path. We headed toward what must have been the lawn and garden section while rank and file Hell Dogs scurried like cockroaches to take up defensive positions.

Gunfire erupted and Fallen Angel—what kind of road name was that, for goodness sakes—abruptly changed directions. We headed to the back of the store, toward the loading dock. His grip on my arm remained punishing. If he'd let go just a little bit, I could twist free, jump on his back, loop my arms over his head and strangle him with the ties binding my wrists. I could go limp, fall to the ground—and probably be yanked along anyway. This bastard wasn't stopping for anything.

"Coward." I ground out the word between gritted teeth.

He stopped so fast I was almost three steps in front of him when I was jerked to a halt and spun around to face him. I worked up a big wad of spit, leaned forward, and got him right in the eye when I spat. Ha! That was the only useful thing Bozo ever taught me.

I just managed to shield my cheek with my shoulder as he swung at me. There was so much power in his punch, I was knocked back about four feet. I landed on my back but managed to curl my neck so my head didn't slam into the concrete floor. If that blow had landed on my face, I'd probably be dead. As it was, I figured my shoulder was broken. I curled up into a ball as I watched his black motorcycle boots approach.

A wolf howled, swear to God. The monster froze, still as death, head swiveling toward the sound. The wolf howled again, the sound a ringing echo above the gunshots and the racket of fights more up close and personal. I raised my head. The dock was empty. Fallen Angel *was* a coward. He'd cut and run.

A huge black shadow barreled past me and it suddenly occurred to me that had I known a real wolf was hunting, I'd have run like hell too. A motorcycle roared to life, followed by a snarl and metal hitting pavement. More snarls. Gunshots. Men yelling. Boots pounding on concrete. More shadows streaming past me in the dark. I didn't move. My shoulder was killing me, the plastic ties bit into my wrists, and my brain had defaulted to "This is all a bad dream" territory.

A man squatted beside me—one I vaguely recognized. Hardass? Something like that. He'd been military. A combat medic. I relaxed slightly and wondered if maybe I had hit my head. Information was not flowing succinctly through my brain.

"Need to check your eyes, babe."

"Okay."

A pen light blinded me for an instant and then it blinked out. I closed my eyes against the tracers and stars dancing in my aftervision. "Am I gonna live?"

His chuckle was low, deep, and hit a girl right where she lived. "Probably."

I heard more men milling around and then I was hoisted off the floor in Hardass's arms and placed on a stack of abandoned pallets. I winced as he jostled my left shoulder.

"Found the breaker box," someone yelled from across the space. Moments later, florescent lights flickered on, illuminating the area. I glanced at the men surrounding me. They all looked...nervous. Like they didn't want to get too close to me. I tucked my chin and sniffed my shirt. I still smelled like piss. Yeah, I couldn't blame them. I wouldn't want to get too close either.

"I'll check your shoulder after I look at the back of your head, babe," Hardass said. "The bitch used a pipe on you and I need to make sure there's no real damage."

"Are you insinuating I have a hard head?"

"You'll need one to live with Gravedigger," someone snickered, his voice so low I'm sure he didn't expect me to hear.

Gravedigger. He wasn't here. Disappointment sat in my stomach like a lump of raw dough. I was positive I'd heard his voice, that he'd insisted he would find me. I realized my cheeks were wet and I brushed away my stupid tears with the backs of my bound hands. The next thing I knew, there was a flash of steel gray and my hands fell apart. The large knife disappeared back into a sheath on Hardass's belt.

"Sorry. Should have done that first."

"Naw," I allowed. "You didn't know if I'd scratch your eyes out…" I stopped speaking as the huge, black wolf padded into the warehouse. "…or not." I finished the phrase, my eyes glued to the animal.

Blood stained his muzzle and he limped a little. I could see what looked like a savage bite on a front leg. Another gash showed through the fur on his side. The slightly hysterical part of my mind wondered if one of the Nightriders had a sidecar on his motorcycle in order to transport the wolf.

Padding closer and halting right in front of me, the wolf sniffed the air. And sneezed. Then he growled. I laughed, the sound coming from that same hysterical corner in the back of my psyche. "Yeah, I know. Stinks, right?"

The wolf reared up and I heard a popping sound what sounded like flesh ripping. My stomach roiled and I gagged as the wolf twisted, morphed, changed. And a naked Gravedigger sat in front of me, a bleeding gash across his ribs, his left forearm bearing the signs of being ravaged by large teeth.

My vision swam. This. Was. Not. Possible.

✿ ✿ ✿ ✿

Gravedigger

I WATCHED SHY closely, waiting for her to bolt. At the moment, she was too busy hyperventilating to consider escape. That would come, though. Fight or flight. And she knew better than to fight me.

"Crazy," she muttered, chin tucked to her chest, eyes refusing to meet mine as she shook her head from side to side.

I pushed her knees apart and hunkered down between them. "Look at me, babe. You aren't insane."

"You're naked."

My laugh burst out. I'd just shifted from my wolf and the fact I was naked was to be expected. Except she didn't know I was a Wolf, and she'd never seen me change until then. Still, this whole situation smacked of irony.

"Yeah, and?"

Her fist lashed out, punching my bare shoulder. "Head injury. I obviously have a concussion. And don't make fun of me."

"Not laughin' at you, babe. Laughin' with you." While Hardy checked her injuries, I cupped her cheek gently. He finished and murmured that he was calling Doc Carson. I leaned my forehead against hers. "I'm sorry."

Because she was my mate, because I was a Wolf and a Nightrider, she'd been sucked into the dark side of my world. Once she was safe, my brothers and I would hunt Hell Dogs. Before we were done, we'd kill every fucker who'd touched her.

"If I'm not crazy or concussed, explain this to me."

"Not here, babe. Once you're safe. Then we'll talk."

"Are you a werewolf?" She searched my face. "Because they don't exist."

"You're right. They don't. Hollywood make believe. I'm a wolf shifter. Big difference."

Laughter tinged with hysteria bubbled from her. "Tell me I'm dreaming."

"Sorry, babe."

"Well…shit."

I caught her as her eyes rolled up and she passed out. *Well shit* was right.

TWENTY-TWO

Shy

I SWAM UP through foggy darkness. I was holding my breath and my heart pounded so hard in my ears I couldn't hear. Where was I? I couldn't move. A heavy, warm weight blanketed me.

"Breathe, baby." The order, one I needed to obey, whispered in my ear.

My body ached. Bad. Almost as bad as those first days in boot camp when the drill instructors drove us to the point we grunts could only faceplant in our bunks at night and sink into exhausted sleep.

Whatever held me down slid away and that gruff voice teased my hearing again. "Dammit, Shy. Breathe."

I inhaled and coughed as air hit my lungs and my ribs expanded.

"Come back to me, baby."

Where had I been that I needed to come back from? I breathed again, and it came easier. Or it did before memories flooded through me, swamping my brain so I stopped breathing again. Rough hands clamped on my shoulders, hauling me up, shaking me until I gulped in another breath. I remembered now.

I remembered the men circling like sharks. I remembered the sound of thunder. I remembered... Opening my eyes, I gazed at the man who had changed *into* that man from a freaking wolf!

Before I could react, I was sitting on the side of a bed, knees spread, head forced down between them.

"Breathe, Shy."

I breathed. The sparklies dazzling my vision settled down. I studied the floor. Concrete painted gray. "You should fire your interior decorator."

A huge sigh of what seemed like relief feathered across my hair. "I'll let you pick out a rug."

"Digger?" Dang. My voice sounded needy. And scared. That's not who I was. I hadn't been that little girl since Digger left me sitting on a bus stop bench. I pushed against his hand and sat up. Time for the truth. "Tell me about Brick."

🐾 🐾 🐾 🐾

Gravedigger

THE LAST THING I expected to come out of Shy's mouth was a demand to know more about Brick McIntire. This woman was my mate and all the crap the mated brothers tossed around about being honest with their mates hit home. Except she didn't know she was mine. And there were some things that none of us spoke of out loud. Like the fact Brick McIntire's wolf skin was nailed to the clubhouse wall.

"There's more important shit to talk about."

She shifted away from me, a subtle move but a message all the same. I stood and walked over to the door, leaning back against it. I'd give her space. For now. She eyed me, speculation written all over her face. She settled back against the headboard, tucking her feet Indian style in front of her. "Like what?"

A hint of defiance. That was good. "Like the three-hundred-pound wolf in the room."

"Yeah...no. I'm not ready to go there."

"Yeah, babe. We're gonna talk about it. It's who I am. What I am."

"There's no such thing as a werewolf."

"We agreed on that before you passed out. As is the fact that I'm not a fucking werewolf. I'm a Wolf." I put emphasis on the word. "The ability to shift from man to wolf is coded in my DNA. It's a recessive gene attached to the Y chromosome." I looked her up and down, letting how much I wanted to fuck her bleed into my eyes. "If you want to talk science, I vote for birds and bees."

She snorted but remained resolute. "I don't believe you."

"You should. Been confirmed by scientists, which is why they're fucking hunting us."

"Hunting...*us*? There's more than one of

you?" I watched the realization wash over her. "Holy hell." She blinked rapidly, her mouth dropping open for a few seconds before she snapped it shut. "That's impossible! You've drugged me. Or hypnotized me. Or...something."

I pulled my T-shirt off over my head and dropped my jeans. My wolf and I both got smug as her eyes dropped to my crotch and widened. Then I shifted. Some of us have a hard time. The process can be long and painful. I've seen some Wolves shift almost effortlessly. My change hurt like a sonavabitch but it didn't take long. That was one of the reasons I was an enforcer and now served as national Sergeant at Arms.

Shy didn't scream but I figure it was only her stubbornness that kept her hands over her mouth and her lips clamped shut. I caught the whimper lodged in her throat. I shook out my fur once the change was complete but didn't move toward the bed. She sat there staring for what seemed like days.

"Holy crap, Wolfman."

Hoping that was a step in the right direction, I sat down. She leaned forward, then swung her legs off the bed and planted her feet on the cold floor before jerking them back. "Definitely getting a rug," she groused. She studied me from the safety of the bed. Silence stretched a little too thin to suit me before she snapped her fingers and said, "Uhm...come here?"

I growled and lay my ears back. She

gulped and shrugged her shoulders. "So, okay. Not a dog." She tilted her head and studied me. "Digger?" I pricked my ears in her direction. "Are you in there? Can you understand what I'm saying? Like a person would?" I huffed and twitched one ear. "Can I pet you?"

I rose to stand on all four feet and very slowly padded to the bed. I wanted to jump up and roll around on her so her scent saturated my fur—an action my wolf was totally on board with—but I didn't want to scare her. Her hand hovered between us so I twisted my head, giving her access to an ear and my neck.

Her fingers landed in my ruff and my fucking wolf wanted to roll over and offer our belly for rubs. I hung onto our dignity because damn if I didn't want the same thing.

"You're so soft," Shy murmured. "And you slept with me in this form. After I—" Her voice cracked. "After I hurt you."

Hurt me? She'd fucking tried to kill me. I pulled against her grip and lifted my muzzle so I could lick her face. Damn she tasted good. I wanted to lick her other places, too, and sink my dick deep into her sweet pussy. I nosed her. *Ready to face the man again?*

"Yes, I—" She broke off the sentence and stared at me. "Did you just *talk?*"

I gave her my best wolfish grin, pulled away, and shifted back to my human form.

"You're naked again."

"And?"

"Well..." She waved her hands around.

"*...naked.*"

My wolfish grin morphed into my human one when I growled, "You're gonna be naked too."

I didn't give her a chance to argue. She was easy to strip down considering the only thing she wore was one of my Harley shirts. I whipped it over her head, baring her. "Fuckin' beautiful."

Shy

MY WHOLE BODY sizzled at his words. Looking into his eyes—gold-flecked green ringed by dark green, I saw the red spark of feral animal that was his wolf. I'd seen it before but I hadn't wanted to acknowledge it. I wasn't sure I was ready to do so now. Trying to wrap my brain around the last twenty-four hours...heck, the last few weeks was more than I could manage at the moment.

Part of me wanted to cover up but the rest of me was all puffed up that this scary-sexy biker thought I was beautiful. And what was totally crazy? I didn't doubt him. He *believed* I was beautiful. But I also knew he was trying to distract me. "Say that again after we've finished talking."

"What's there to talk about?" He grabbed my calves and yanked. Two seconds later, I was flat on my back, legs spread, with Digger's head buried between my thighs. His mouth clamped down on me, sucking, tasting, nipping. He raised his head, those feral eyes gone over to wolf. "Done talkin', babe. Time for fuckin'."

Then he lowered his head and went back to eating me. He stroked his tongue across my center and I muffled my scream with a pillow. I felt his teeth on my clit. I wanted him to stop. I wanted him to keep doing this forever. My brain stopped working as instinct took over. I squirmed, lifting my hips to his mouth.

"Hungry cunt," he murmured against my quivering flesh. "Just the way I want you."

He shoved his shoulders under my thighs so my knees draped over them. His hands cupped my butt cheeks, squeezing and lifting as he feasted on me. He wasn't the only one starving for this. Heat and tension, fierce emotion and furious need all coiled tight within me.

"Pleasepleasepleaseplease." Someone begged in a torn whisper. Me. That someone was me. Begging. I broke, a wave of ecstasy drowning me. I couldn't breathe. Couldn't move. Couldn't think. But I felt. I felt *everything*.

Digger huffed out a satisfied grunt. If I'd had the energy, I would have slugged the smug grin off his face. If I could have formed words, I would have told him to go to hell. He dragged his tongue through my sex one final time, lapping up the last of my climax.

He rubbed his chin up my sensitized skin, his stubble leaving burning marks in his wake. "Now it's time to get serious." The wicked light in his eyes set my body on fire.

"No," I managed to choke out. "Can't take any more."

"You can," he disagreed. "You will."

He slid up my body, stopping to suck on both of my breasts as one hand dropped to cup me, his fingers teasing and tormenting my sex. I was so swollen down there that pain mixed with pleasure, and pleasure won out. Arching against him, I swallowed his laughter as his mouth claimed mine.

Digger's body was warm skin over hard muscle and his whole weight stretched over me. The hair on his chest abraded my nipples and they pebbled against him. His fingers stroked in and out of me and another climax built in my core. Then I was empty. I cried out but he was already shifting his weight and then his cock—his huge, wonderful cock pushed inside me, burying all the way, his tight balls slapping against the curve of my butt.

I had to be out of my mind. This man wasn't human. But the things he did to my body, the way he made me feel? He gripped my butt, lifting, changing the angle and I lost all pretense at control. My lips found his chest, my tongue lapping at the hair covering the ridged muscles, and without a thought to the consequences, my teeth fastened on his skin and bit down.

He growled, holding my head against his skin, forcing my teeth deeper and then his mouth latched onto the muscle between my neck and my shoulder and he bit down. God, it hurt but I shattered beneath his hold as his cock plunged in and out of me in a frenzied rhythm.

I came a third time before he released the bite and pushed up so he could see my face. His wolf watched me, golden green fire in his eyes. "Mine," he snarled, still more wolf than man. "My mate. Forever."

Real wolves supposedly did that. Mated forever. Why would I think this wild man was any different? But how could I give my heart and soul to the man who had shaped my entire life? My brain churned, too closely resembling handfuls of stuff tossed into a blender. That one seminal event in my childhood made me what I was today…who I was today.

"Stop." I pushed against the solid wall of his chest. I had to figure this out and with his cock filling me, his hands inciting my body to another orgasm, I couldn't think.

"No." He pulled out and I whimpered at the loss. What was wrong with me? Then I was up and flying and positioned on my elbows and knees, butt in the air. Before I could utter another word, he was buried balls deep in my sex once more. He slammed into me and I braced my hands against the headboard, using a pillow to cushion my head.

Fingers swiped between us and then he spread my butt cheeks, teasing my rear entrance with a finger coated in my cum.

Between one stroke of his cock and the next, he pushed a finger into me. I whimpered again from the sheer pleasure of it. Then he had two fingers in me and they set up a counter rhythm to his cock. No more thinking. Only feeling. Only emotion.

I came again, every muscle clamping down. Digger swore but he kept working me with cock and fingers. Leaning over my back, he kissed the nape of my neck.

"So fucking good, baby."

Yes. I wanted to melt, my whole body so limp I couldn't quite comprehend why I was still upright.

"One more, baby girl."

One more? How was that even possible? Then his fingers found my clit. I spiraled out of control within moments. I was sobbing and shaking as I came. He stroked deep inside me. Once. Twice. A few more times and then I felt the hot splash of his cum filling me. I fell over the edge again and when I came down, I was in his arms, surrounded by all the hard, male muscle and musk that was my...mate.

TWENTY-THREE

Gravedigger

I LAY AWAKE for hours watching Shy sleep. My wolf was curled up inside me, sated and content. He'd tasted her blood when we marked her and found her sweetness satisfying. I'd never wanted a mate—thinking I'd lost my best shot at finding the one. Swore I would never fall into a night full of the crazy that was being moonstruck. Watching others fall into it for life was cause for jeering and drinking and finding a sweet butt to fuck in celebration that it wasn't me. I liked my women compliant and knowing when to keep their mouths shut.

Smothering my laugh, I admitted to myself that I was so fucked. There wasn't a compliant bone in Shy's body. At least not until I'd made her come so many times she could no longer think. Like that was a chore. She was brash, courageous, and ours—the wolf and me.

She had curves because skinny women weren't my thing but lean muscle formed those curves. My woman could hold her own and given the shit that hit the club more often than not, I'd be in the middle of it. She'd have to be able to take care of herself.

My wolf growled at that. We were supposed to take care of her, guard her, keep her safe. He wasn't quite so content now. He wanted to hunt down those sons of bitches who had hurt her. Their stench had still been on her when I brought her back to the clubhouse. Thankfully, she remained unconscious while we dealt with the Hell Dogs who hadn't escaped. I'd stripped her down and we showered before she woke up in my bed. Right where she would be from now on.

The knock on the door was soft, as was the voice calling my name. Easy. What the hell? I disentangled from Shy and padded naked to the door. Stepping outside, I closed it behind me.

"This better be fuckin' important, bro."

Easy was my back-up enforcer and while his name implied his attitude, the guy was hard as steel underneath. "We have a line on another group of Hell Dogs in our territory. Thought we'd pay 'em a visit while they're sleeping off their drunk. Figured you'd want in on the action."

"Hell, yeah. I'll be out front in five."

I was dressed in two and took a minute to find paper and a pen. I left a note lying on Shy's phone: *Club business. I'll be back.*

I didn't kiss her. If I did, I'd never leave.

Shy

I WOKE UP when I heard a bunch of motorcycles fire up. Digger's side of the bed was still warm, something I discovered when I carefully stretched my legs. I wasn't exactly sore down there, but Digger had definitely worked me over last night. I very carefully rotated my shoulder. Evidently, the Club's doctor had checked me over. Nothing broken or sprained, just bone-deep bruising. Happily exhausted, I rolled into the warm spot that smelled of him and fell back asleep. The next time I surfaced, his side of the bed was still empty. While I was disappointed and a little nervous, I wasn't worried. Not exactly. Yes, I was in his room at the Barracks and he wasn't here, but my shoulder ached from where he'd bitten me. Claimed me. As his mate. I was still a little freaked out about that.

Okay. I was a lot freaked out. The dang man turned into a wolf. A big, beautiful black wolf. If I smoked grass, I'd say I'd gotten hold of some primo shit. I didn't do drugs. My phone pinged to let me know I'd gotten an email, and I found the note as I reached for it.

Club business. What did that mean? My stomach growled and I decided to get cleaned up and go in search of food. First things first.

Twenty minutes later, I was dressed in a pair of jeans I'd left behind and one of Digger's Harley T-shirts. I'd just reached for the doorknob when someone knocked.

"Yeah?"

"Shiane?" It was a female voice. Thinking

about the sweet butt who'd clobbered me at the gas pump, I didn't open the door.

"Yeah, what do you want?"

"You might not remember me. I'm Ginger, Radar's old lady."

Still uneasy, I cracked the door open but blocked it with my body. The redhead flashed me a beaming smile. "There's club business going down so some of us are going out for breakfast. Wanna come?"

My stomach growled again, causing her to laugh. "I'll take that as a yes. C'mon."

I stepped into the hall and shut the door, then hesitated. Should I lock it? I didn't want to just wander off and leave it accessible but I didn't have a key. Ginger noticed my dilemma.

"No one will bother Gravedigger's room. The only time they lock doors is when they don't want someone barging in." She rolled her eyes and laughed again. "Or someone getting out."

"Do you live here with…Radar?" Her laughter was so full of joy I couldn't help but grin. "I'll take that as a no."

"We have a house but Radar keeps a room here. All the brothers do." Her cheeks pinkened. "And yeah, when we get in a…mood, we'll crash here." She held the door for me, and as I stepped out, I saw several of the other old ladies that I recognized. Sam, the blonde who'd taken me home after Digger's and my fight, dangled a key chain.

"I stole the keys to the Russian's

Hummer!"

Giggling like a girl posse at a boy band concert, the whole group charged across the courtyard to the burly black Hummer parked beside one of the garage buildings. We climbed inside, with Sam, who I remembered was Easy's old lady, settling into the driver's seat. Ginger called shotgun. That left Lainey, who was with Hollywood, and Leigh in the backseat with me. I hadn't really met Leigh other than that tense moment during the raid. Her old man was a brother called Smoke. I wasn't sure if I'd met him yet or not.

"We need a big breakfast," Ginger declared, turning around to face the rest of us. "Where should we go?"

"Momma's," Leigh and Lainey shouted in unison.

Ginger pouted. "The guys always take us there. Let's go somewhere nice."

"That means we'd all have to change clothes," Sam pointed out as she waved merrily at the two men standing next to the gate. One of them already had his phone up to his ear.

"Uhm…" I began hesitantly. "Are we gonna be in trouble for taking the Hummer?"

The four women exchanged glances, then burst into laughter. "If the Russian gets pissy, I'll tell him he can't have Noni time. I swear that kid has him wrapped around her little finger."

"So Noni is your and Easy's daughter?"

That's all it took. I got the full version of

how Sam and Easy met, what the Hell Dogs did to her twin, how she and Easy adopted her niece and nephew, how the Dogs took her, and way more TMI stuff than I wanted. Then Lainey and Leigh told their stories. By the time they'd finished, Sam was parking at a diner built out of boxcars. A neon sign on the top of the building spelled out "Momma's Kitchen" one letter at a time then flashed the full name. A second neon sign in the window read, "Open 24/7." No LED lights for this place. It was all original neon.

We spilled in through the door and a waitress straight from central casting stubbed out a cigarette in the ashtray by her elbow. She pointed a finger at each of my companions, reciting their drink choices. Then she came to me.

"You're new. What's your poison?"

"Coffee. And ice water."

"Corner booth, girls."

"And keep the noise level down," a gruff voice yelled from behind the cut-through to the kitchen.

"Aye-aye, Momma!" Sam saluted smartly and led the way to the large round booth tucked into the back corner.

"Let me guess," I said. "Regulars?"

They laughed and nodded but no one said anything while the waitress delivered our drinks. She gave the fisheye to each old lady, and said, "Y'all want your usual?" Everyone nodded before she turned that look on me. "What about you, new girl?"

I looked for a menu but didn't see one so I made noncommittal if questioning sounds in my throat.

"The buttermilk pancakes are to die for," Sam murmured in my ear.

That was easy. "I'll have the same as her." I pointed at Sam.

"The Works it is," the waitress tossed back over her shoulder.

"The Works?" I gave big eyes to Sam.

"Stack of pancakes, two eggs over easy, medium bacon, link sausage, and hash browns."

My stomach growled again. Yeah, I could handle that much food. The small talk continued until our orders arrived. Once Alice—I finally caught a glimpse of her name tag—retreated back behind the counter, all eyes turned to me.

"So," Sam started. "You tried to gut Gravedigger."

I suddenly wasn't very hungry after all.

Gravedigger

THE HOUSE BELONGED to the club whore who'd set up Shy. She'd disappeared during the rescue, but we'd left a prospect to watch her place, as well as the empty warehouse store. He's the one who'd called Easy. The place looked deserted as we rolled up and our prospect was nowhere to be found.

My gut clenched as we approached the house. The rusted iron stench of old blood filled the place like someone had set off a bug bomb. Smoke, who'd gone around the side, whistled. With a gloved hand, Easy tried the door. It was unlocked and opened at his touch.

He stepped inside, with me covering his back. Hollywood, Domino, and the Russian followed in quick succession. Smoke and Gunner, who'd become our national nomad once Smoke mated, remained outside to cover.

I expected to find our prospect. We found the woman. The Hell Dogs hadn't been kind. I wanted her dead for what she'd done to Shy, but I would have killed her quick. The Hell Dogs played with their food like cats. Someone had stapled—literally—a note to her forehead.

"We have the pup you call Rebel. Come and get him."

Shy

THE SOUND OF Harley pipes saved me. We all craned our necks to look out the window to see who was coming. It was one of the guys from the gate and two older bikers I didn't recognize. The old ladies exchanged worried looks.

"That's Hoss and Deadhead with Booker," Ginger said. "If the Topeka prez is here, something big is going down and the guys were serious about us being on lock down." Her gaze fell back on me, and the others followed suit.

"Gotta be the Hell Dogs." Sam's blue eyes were coated in frost. "I hope they find those bastards and wipe them off the face of the earth."

Something twisted in my gut and I wanted to vomit. Hate. So much hate. And anger. I looked up, sweat beading on my upper lip as I fought back nausea. The old ladies weren't paying me any attention now, their eyes glued to the front door. Not them. This feeling wasn't coming from them.

I gagged, drawing their attention again. I managed to choke out, "Bathroom?"

Lainey pointed toward a dark hallway. "I'll come with—"

I slapped my hand over my mouth and bolted, disappearing into the shadows as the two big bikers walked through the entrance. I saw the illuminated exit sign and didn't even slow down. It wasn't alarmed—thank God— and I was out in the sunshine before I stopped to think.

Gravedigger. I had to get to him. Whatever was cramping my stomach had to do with him. His injury maybe? I wasn't sure. I was sure of only one thing—he was hurt and I had to get to him. I looked around for a car to steal. Nothing. Creeping to the front corner of the diner, I checked the parking lot. The prospect called Booker stood next to his bike, his eyes glued to the door of Momma's. I noticed two things: he had a pistol and the keys to his bike were still in the ignition.

I came in hard and fast. The kid never had a chance. Taking him by surprise, I put him on the ground, disarmed him, and was straddling his Harley before he could roll over. I was halfway down the block before the others erupted from the front door. Part of me felt bad for Booker. He'd be disciplined, but if he wanted to be an outlaw biker, he'd take it.

Me? If I survived this insanity, I'd probably be in the same cell with him. I didn't care. My old man needed me, and there wasn't a damn thing anyone could do to stop me from getting to him.

Somehow, I knew exactly where he was. Not the address or anything, just the direction. It was like a pulse in my head—turn here, drive fast, turn left, drive faster. I sensed that the Hummer and the Nightriders from the diner were on my tail. Didn't matter. Nothing mattered except getting to Gravedigger.

Gravedigger

ACCORDING TO THE Russian, Rebel was still alive. As our Alpha, the man had an uncanny sense about each of us. I glanced at him and took an instinctive step backwards. His anger was as black as obsidian, and just as cold and sharp. I assessed our group.

The Russian. Hardass. Easy. Smoke. Gunner. Me. The top of the food chain in the national chapter. Next tier down, there was Domino, Wizard, Hollywood, Sandhog, and Brass. Rounding out our numbers were Jax, Warlock, and Midnight from the KC, Kansas chapter. Fourteen Wolves. I glanced at Smoke. The bastard was as elusive as his namesake. He was returning from scouting the building.

Built of concrete blocks, it sat on the edge of a dying industrial area. Not quite dilapidated, it still looked worse for the wear. A chain-link fence with barb wire strung along the top circled part of the place. The parking lot was wide open. Only a handful of bikes were parked out front.

Smoke held death in his eyes as he reported to the Russian. "Rebel's alive and they're keeping him conscious. Back room, like a shop area. There are eight Dogs with him. All human."

We all exchanged looks. The Hell Dogs took in scum and only about a third of them were Wolves but their national prez, the guy who called himself Fallen Angel, was a Wolf.

"Cannon fodder," Gunner spat.

Nodding, Smoke continued. "There are ten more, including two Wolves, hunkered down in what might have been a break room. They're drinking, passing around bottles of Jack and Jose."

Jack Daniel's and Jose Cuervo. Whiskey and tequila for breakfast. Only the Wolves would be sober. So far the odds weren't even close to being interesting.

"The rest of the bikes are tucked up all nice and neat in an outbuilding. There are forty-two. I rigged the place to blow. That should pull some of the rats out of their hidey-holes. I didn't get eyes on all of them. There are pockets of them throughout the building. Probably some hiding up in the drop ceiling."

"Shame about losing all the bikes," Brass groused.

Smoke's grin was all-knowing. "Rigged the building, not the bikes. We can salvage."

Brass smothered a laugh. "I do like the way you think, my man."

The hard edges returned to Smoke's face. "No sign of the fuckin' Angel."

The Russian lifted one shoulder in a very Slavic shrug. "He is a coward. He will sacrifice his brothers while he tucks his tail and runs. Another day."

That was a promise we all intended to keep.

TWENTY-FOUR

Gravedigger

DOMINO, WIZARD, and Midnight stripped and shifted into their wolves. The rest of us were armed with enough firepower to take down a small army. We all had good noses but nothing compared when we were in wolf form. Those who changed would scout for the Hell Dogs who were hiding. Plus, facing down a snarling wolf was piss-in-your-pants scary to a full human. I grinned, knowing the humor didn't reach my eyes. My wolf was looking out of them. These sons of bitches had taken our mate. Hurt her. And they'd hurt our brother. Time for them to die.

The alarm sounded just as Gunner, Brass, and I breached the shop area through a metal door. The Dogs all jumped to their feet. One swung a pistol toward Rebel while the others opened fire on us. I took down the one. Gunner and Brass annihilated the others.

Hardy followed us in, a giant medical pack swinging from one hand. He immediately set to work on Rebel. We'd need a vehicle to transport him. We'd put the old ladies on lock down at the clubhouse, leaving Hoss and some of our provisionals, backed up by the Topeka Nightriders, on guard duty. I grabbed my phone and speed dialed Hoss to send the van while Hardy checked the kid's injuries.

"There's a problem with the old ladies," Hoss growled through my phone's speaker. Hollywood had just entered from another door and he froze. "They decided that we weren't serious about them being on lock down. They stole the Russian's Hummer and headed to Momma's for fucking breakfast. Almost ran over Booker and that new prospect, Daltrey."

"And?"

"We caught up to them but there's a problem with your girl, Gravedigger."

The men around me backed up as my wolf surged to the surface. My voice was barely human as I growled out, "Problem?"

Hoss's voice was just as growly. "She stole Booker's bike and weapon. The old ladies took off after her in the Hummer. We're on their tail and have reinforcements on the way. Thing is, boss, it looks like they're headed straight for you."

My wolf sat down, head cocked like he was listening.

I'm coming.

That was Shy's voice in my head. *What the fuck?*

Don't what the fuck me. You're hurt.

Hollywood had a stupid grin on his face. "Mating bond," he explained. "The Russian is going to be pissed as hell but at least the Hummer will be here to take Rebel to Doc's clinic. We need to clear out the cockroaches before the girls get here."

That's when the shooting started out front.

Shy

MAYBE I SHOULD have thought a bit more clearly about current circumstances. I'd reacted blindly, figuring out that Digger's *club business* meant he might get hurt again. Something in me just snapped. I had to get to him. So I'd been stupid. And I rode straight into an ambush. Not only that, I'd led the other old ladies into the same trap.

There were four wolves fighting on the side of the building. None of them was my man. The first bullet pinged off the Harley's motor and I laid it down. The road rash was gonna hurt if I survived—and if Digger didn't kill me. I could feel his anger—and his fear— like a physical touch.

Bullets flew. I stayed hunkered down behind the big bike. Checking the clip in the pistol I'd lifted from the provisional, I realized I had a Glock 37, which was a .45 caliber pistol with ten bullets. And I was in the middle of a hot fire-fight. With little to no cover. Yeah, my sign would read "STUPID," in all capital letters.

I heard boots scuff behind me. Rolling over, I pulled the trigger. Once. The bullet caught the guy just above his breastbone. He crumpled, his own weapon skittering across the broken concrete. I snaked over and grabbed it, automatically checking the magazine. Great. I now had a total of fifteen shots. At least I could go down with a fight. Brakes screeched behind me, followed by the roar of Harleys, way more than just the two from the diner. Lord but I hoped they were the good guys.

A howl caught my attention. The wolves no longer fought. Two were down and I prayed they weren't Nightriders. I'd learned from the old ladies that Digger wasn't the only Wolf. That there were Wolves in the Hell Dogs? That was something I didn't want to think about, despite the fight going on.

Windows in the building shattered, but I couldn't tell if it was from outside gunfire or whether those inside broke them out. Then I heard the voice that turned my body to jelly.

"You keep your fuckin' head down, Shiane Rourke. You hear me?"

Gravedigger

SHY HEARD ME. She flipped me the bird. Fuckin' cute but I was going to turn her over my knee and blister her ass once we were done with the Dogs. She'd at least thought to arm herself. The Hummer was half a block down the road. Hoss, Sandhog, and other brothers were taking cover around and near it. The damn thing was armor-plated so the old ladies were safe. For the time being. Once my brothers got hold of them...I'd bet even money that not one of them would be sitting comfortably come tomorrow.

"Shit." Gunner watched something out the window he was covering. "Movement on the left. They're trying to get to her, using the weeds along the fence as cover."

The Russian glanced through another window. "Wizard, Domino, and Midnight are stalking them. Are we sure this building is clear?"

We all answered in the affirmative. Hardy appeared, his face devoid of emotion. "The kid's bleeding internally. We need to get him to Doc's ASAP, Russki."

"Keep him alive, Hardy. We will take care of the rest."

Hardy disappeared back down the hallway. The Russian smiled and I swear every last one of us shivered. "There are twenty-three of them left. We are more than a match." His gaze fell on Smoke. "It is time."

Smoke pulled a small electronic device from a pocket and pressed it. Three seconds later, thunder like that accompanying a direct lightning strike filled the air, followed by a rumble that shook the ground. Dust filtered down from the ceiling, not that anyone was left inside to notice. We were all out in the parking lot, guns blazing.

Three wolves fell on a group of Hell Dogs

hunkered down in the weeds. They'd stopped trying to get to Shy the moment the explosion registered. The rest were caught in the direct fire we and our reinforcements laid down. The shoot-out was over in seconds, not that I was paying much attention. I was focused on one thing—getting to my mate. She'd be my patched property by nightfall.

"What the hell are you doing here, Shy?"

Shy

DIGGER DID NOT look very happy to see me. Not sure I could blame him, given that he'd just walked through a hail of bullets to get to me. This man had risked his life more than once to rescue me. To free me from the past. Why the big scary-sexy biker fell for me, I didn't know. But he had. And I took the fall with him. Hard.

Gravedigger. Shane. Digger. The man who turned into a wolf. The Wolf who loved me. I smiled cheekily and answered, my voice teasing. "I missed you?"

He grabbed me and kissed me hard, kissed me like there would never be another tomorrow. His heart slowed down, taking mine with it until our heartbeats pulsed in perfect synchronization. My old man. My mate. My everything. "Did you miss me?"

"Damn straight, babe, but this shit has to stop."

EPILOGUE

Gravedigger

THE NEXT FEW hours were crazy. Easy's old lady, Sam, helped Hardy with Rebel. They loaded the provisional into the back of the Hummer. Lainey and Ginger tried to bully Shy into leaving with them. When that didn't work, they bribed her by letting her drive. Leigh, Smoke's old lady, stayed behind. She'd been an arson investigator down in Dallas before they mated. She'd help with the cover-up.

Brass made a call and within twenty minutes, a semi-truck and enclosed trailer appeared. All the bikes belonging to the Hell Dogs were trundled on board. Brass ran Chrome, the custom garage the club owned. Within forty-eight hours, most of the bikes would be stripped and parted out, the rest waiting to be altered and customized.

Hell Dog bodies, including the two Wolves' bodies, still in wolf form, were dragged into the building. Smoke and Leigh would rig the place to burn, ensuring it looked like an accident—and one that spread to the outbuilding.

The fact it was Sunday kept us from

being discovered. That, and most of the surrounding area had been abandoned. Not even the cops patrolled routinely. Final count was forty-two Hell Dogs dead. Besides Rebel, a few of the brothers took minor injuries. A quick disinfection and a change and the injured would be fine. Hell, they were all in better shape than me.

Leave it to me to fall for a blood-thirsty ex-Army cop with long brown hair, big brown eyes, and a body made to fit mine. We left the scene of the ambush in small groups, despite the urge to ride as a full pack. Such a show of force would alert the cops. Shy was on my mind and my dick was throbbing with the need to be inside her. The others hadn't lied about the frenzy that came with being moonstruck. I had a stop to make before I could claim my mate again.

When I finally walked into the clubhouse. Shy was there, sitting at the bar. She swiveled the moment I walked in. I stalked toward her but she stood—or sat, since she didn't get off the stool she occupied—her ground. Domino slouched on the other side of the bar. He'd just put an opened long-neck beer in front her. He backed away, leaning against the back bar, arms folded across his chest, grinning like a fool.

Shy's face softened as she watched me, but her eyes glinted with the same sexual heat I felt. First things first. I caged her against the bar and shook out the leather bundle I carried. She was damn well going to wear my property patch. I draped it over her shoulders and waited. Her arms slipped through the vest's armholes, then came around my neck. Her lips met mine in a crushing kiss.

Yes. Her assent exploded in my mind.

Hell yeah. My mate. My woman. My fuckin' old lady.

Her legs joined her arms by wrapping around my waist and I hoisted her off the bar stool. She broke our kiss long enough to yell, "I'm going to go fuck my old man now."

We left the clubhouse to a round of cheering gibes. Once in my room, I put her down only long enough to strip our clothes off. She fell back on the bed, taking me down on top of her.

"Inside me," she ordered.

I obeyed, sinking into her hot, welcoming pussy. My wolf chuffed inside me, settling into the glow that was our mate. Home. Somehow, I'd known my fate was tied to that little girl so many years before. On that bloody night, I found my identity and my brothers. And my forever with a woman called Shy, who was anything but.

🐾 🐾 🐾 🐾

Dear Reader:

If this is your first Nightrider book, I hope you'll go back and read their story from the beginning. This won't be the last book in the series, either. Why? It's not a secret to the cool folks who hang out with me on social media. I have an abiding love of well-written MC books. I blame Joanna Wylde and Kristen Ashley for my addiction. Because, ya know? There's just something about finding the protective side of a really badass alpha male. I was all in when the world of my Moonstruck Wolves took a detour into the gritty and oft-times violent lives of the Nightriders. These outlaw MC brothers thundered out of the dark into my imagination, and above the roar of their Harleys, they introduced themselves. And I fell for them. Hard!

I wasn't ready for Gravedigger's story, and in fact, had an entirely different heroine planned for him. Then Shy walked in, sat down and told me off. What could I do but write their story?

This world isn't for everyone. The Nightriders are an outlaw motorcycle club. Their enemies think nothing of rape, torture, and murder. If readers are sensitive to these themes, this is not the series for them.

Thank you for visiting my worlds. The door is always open so don't be a stranger. Happy reading!

~Silver James

🐾 🐾 🐾 🐾

Thank you for reading this book!

Reviews and word of mouth help other readers find books to read. I appreciate every review. Please consider leaving one on Amazon, Goodreads, and/or on the book review site of your choice. If this is your first Nightrider book, please check out my other stories in this series as well as the books in my Moonstruck world, my Urban Fantasy series Penumbra Papers, or my sexy contemporary series from Harlequin, Red Dirt Royalty. Keep reading for the list of all my titles.

TITLES BY SILVER JAMES

Paranormal Romance

MOONSTRUCK WOLVES

In the beginning, there were the Wolves of Army Special SciOps Unit 69...

Moonstruck Genesis:
Moonstruck: Secrets
(Contains the books Blood Moon and Bad Moon plus additional chapters and cut scenes)
Moonstruck: Lies
(Contains the books Hunter's Moon and Wolf Moon plus additional chapters and cut scenes)
Coming soon:
Moonstruck: Betrayal
Moonstruck: Retribution

Moonstruck:
*Blood Moon – Book 1
*Bad Moon – Book 2
*Hunter's Moon – Book 3
*Wolf Moon – Book 4
*Bride's Moon – Book 5
*Rogue Moon – Book 6
*Christmas Moon – A Moonstruck Novella
(#7)

*Blue Moon – Book 8
*Moon Shot – Book 9
(A Moonstruck/Hard Target Crossover Novel)

Series set in the Moonstruck World:

Hard Target

Double Cross – Book 1
**Double Trouble
(A Hard Target companion novella set in Roxanne St. Claire's Barefoot Bay World)

Welcome to the darkest side of the Moonstruck world. Not every Wolf walks the straight and narrow like the Wolves of the 69th. Gritty, earthy, and violent, rogue Wolves run on the criminal side of society. Gun running, strip clubs, bounty hunters, the Nightriders live their lives in the outlaw 1%. There's sex, violence, and violent sex, and sometimes, a Wolf smacks up against the woman destined to turn him moonstruck...

Nightriders MC
Night Shift – Book 1
*Remember the Night – #1.5
Night Moves – Book 2
Night Fire – Book 3
Night Fall – Book 4

Other Books set in the Moonstruck World:

Susan Stoker's Worlds
**Rescue Moon
**SEAL Moon
**Assassin's Moon
Under the Assassin's Moon

Elle James Brotherhood Protector World
**Montana Moon

Moonstruck Wolf
**Blood & Fire (revised)
**Crash & Burn (revised)

Urban Fantasy

PENUMBRA PAPERS

That Ol' Black Magic
Season of the Witch
The Devil's Cut
The Sound of Silence

Contemporary Romance

From Harlequin Desire

Red Dirt Royalty

Cowgirls Don't Cry
The Cowgirl's Little Secret
The Boss and His Cowgirl
Convenient Cowgirl Bride
Redeemed by the Cowgirl
Claiming the Cowgirl's Baby
The Cowboy's Christmas Proposition
Billionaire Country
RDR #9 coming May 2010

From Wild Rose Press:

Time Travel Paranormal

Faerie Reign
Faerie Fate
Faerie Fire
Faerie Fool
*Faerie Reign
(Digital 3-book boxed set at a special price)
*Faerie Faith (Twelve Brides of Christmas)

Contemporary Romance

Class of '85 Reunion Series:
*Fairy Tales Can Come True
*Promises, Promises

Dearly Beloved Series:
*Best Laid Plans

Paranormal Noir

Other Novella:
*Café Midnight
(Paranormal Noir Mystery)

*Available in digital format only
**Books previously published in worlds created by other authors that have been, republished under a revision or reassignment of rights

ABOUT THE AUTHOR

 Silver James likes to take walks on the wild side and coffee. Okay. She loves coffee. LOTS of coffee. Warning: Her Muse, Iffy, runs with scissors and can be quite dangerous. She's the author of four award-winning series: Nightriders MC, Moonstruck, The Penumbra Papers, and Red Dirt Royalty. She's been a military officer's wife, mother, and has worked in the legal field, fire service, and law enforcement. Now retired from the "real world," she lives in Oklahoma and spends her days at the computer with two rescued Newfoundland dogs, the cats who rule them all, and the myriad characters living in her imagination. She writes dark paranormal romantic thrillers, urban fantasy, and sexy contemporary romance for Harlequin Desire.

To find out more about Silver and her books, visit her website at **www.silverjames.com** where you can sign up for her newsletter, get info on all her books, and other fun things. You can also track her down (and follow her!) on Facebook at Silver James Romance, Instagram at Author Silver James, Twitter at @SilverJames_, and Pinterest at Silver James.